Facing the World

Horatio Alger, Jr.

TABLE OF CONTENTS

PREFACE

CHAPTER I

CHAPTER II

CHAPTER III

CHAPTER IV

CHAPTER V

CHAPTER VI

CHAPTER VII

CHAPTER VIII

CHAPTER IX

CHAPTER X

CHAPTER XI

CHAPTER XII

CHAPTER XIII

CHAPTER XIV

CHAPTER XV

CHAPTER XVI

CONCLUSION

PREFACE

Horatio Alger, Jr., in "Facing the World," gives us as his hero a boy whose parents have both died and the man appointed as his guardian is unjust and unkind to him. In desperation he runs away and is very fortunate in finding a true friend in a man who aids him and makes him his helper in his work as magician.

They travel over the country and have many interesting experiences, some narrow escapes and thrilling adventures.

CHAPTER I

HARRY RECEIVES A LETTER

"Here's a letter for you, Harry," said George Howard. "I was passing the hotel on my way home from school when Abner Potts called out to me from the piazza, and asked me to bring it."

The speaker was a bright, round-faced boy of ten. The boy whom he addressed was five or six years older. Only a week previous he had lost his father, and as the family consisted only of these two, he was left, so far as near relatives were concerned, alone in the world. Immediately after the funeral he had been invited home by Mr. Benjamin Howard, a friend of his father, but in no manner connected with him by ties of relationship.

"You can stay here as long as you like, Harry," said Mr. Howard, kindly. "It will take you some time to form your plans, perhaps, and George will be glad to have your company."

"Thank you, Mr. Howard," said Harry, gratefully.

"Shall you look for some employment here?"

"No; my father has a second cousin in Colebrook, named John Fox. Before he died he advised me to write to Mr. Fox, and go to his house if I should receive an invitation."

"I hope for your sake, he will prove a good man. What is his business?"

"I don't know, nor did my father. All I know is, that he is considered a prosperous man. This letter is from him."

It was inclosed in a brown envelope, and ran as follows:

"HARRY VANE: I have received your letter saying that your father wants me to be your guardeen. I don't know as I have any objections, bein' a business man it will come easy to me, and I think your father was wise to seleck me. I am reddy to receave you any time. You will come to Bolton on the cars. That is eight miles from here, and there is a stage that meats the trane. It wouldn't do you any harm to walk, but boys ain't so active as they were in my young days. The stage fare is fifty cents, which I shall expect you to pay yourself, if you ride.

"There is one thing you don't say anything about—how much proparty your pa left. I hope it is a good round sum, and I will take good care of it for you. Ennybody round here will tell you that John Fox is a good man of business, and about as sharp as most people. Mrs. Fox will be glad to see you, and my boy, Joel, will be glad to have someone to keep him company. He is about sixteen years old. You don't say how old you are, but from your letter I surmise that you are as much as that. You will find a happy united famerly, consistin' of me and my wife, Joel and his sister, Sally. Sally is fourteen, just two years younger than Joel. We live in a comfortable way, but we don't gorge ourselves on rich, unhelthy food. No more at present. Yours to command,

"JOHN FOX."

Harry smiled more than once as he read this letter.

"Your relative isn't strong on spelling," remarked Mr. Howard, as he laid the letter on the table.

"No, sir; but he appears to be strong on economy. It is a comfort to know that I shall not be injured by 'rich, unhelthy food.'"

"When do you mean to start for Colebrook?" asked Mr. Howard.

"To-morrow morning. I have been looking at a railroad guide, and I find it will bring me to Colebrook in time for supper."

"We should be glad to have you stay with us as long as possible, Harry."

"Thank you, Mr. Howard, I don't doubt that, but the struggle of life is before me, and I may as well enter upon it at once."

At four o'clock in the afternoon the conductor of the train on which Harry was a passenger called out Bolton.

Harry snatched up his carpetbag, and made his way to the door, for this was the place where he was to take the stage for Colebrook.

Two other passengers got out at the same time. One was an elderly man, and the other a young man of twenty-five. They appeared to be father and son, and, as Harry learned afterward they were engaged in farming.

"Any passengers for Colebrook?" inquired the driver of the old-fashioned Concord stage, which was drawn up beside the platform.

"There's Obed and me," said the old farmer.

"May I ride on the seat with you?" asked Harry of the driver.

"Sartain. Where are you going?"

"To Colebrook."

"Then this is your team."

Harry climbed up with a boy's activity, and sat down on the broad seat, congratulating himself that he would have a chance to see the country, and breathe better air than those confined inside.

Soon the driver sat down on the box beside him, and started the horses.

"You're a stranger, ain't you?" he remarked, with an inquisitive glance at his young traveling companion.

"Yes; I've never been here before."

"Are you going to the tavern?"

"No; I'm going to the house of Mr. John Fox. Do you know him?"

"I reckon everybody round here knows John Fox."

"I don't know him. He is to be my guardian."

"Sho! You'll have a queer guardeen."

"Why queer?"

"The fact is, old John'll cheat you out of your eye teeth ef he gets a chance. He's about the sharpest man round."

"He can't cheat me out of much," returned Harry, not especially reassured by this remark.

"What is the business of Mr. Fox?"

"Well, he's got some land, but he makes his livin' chiefly by tradin' hosses, auctioneerin', and such like."

"What sort of a woman is Mrs. Fox?"

"She's a good match for the old man. She's about as mean as he is."

"Mr. Fox wrote me that he had two children."

"Yes, there's Joel—he's about your age. He's a chip of the old block—red-headed and freckled, just like the old man. I don't believe Joel ever spent a cent in his life. He hangs on to money as tight as ef his life depended on it."

"There's a girl, too, isn't there?"

"Yes, Sally. She looks like her ma, except she's red-headed like her pa."

"I'm glad to know something of the family, but I'm afraid I shan't enjoy myself very much among the Foxes."

With such conversation Harry beguiled the way. On the whole, he enjoyed the ride. There were hills and here and there the road ran through the woods. He could hear the singing of birds, and, notwithstanding what he had heard he felt in good spirits.

At length the stage entered the village of Colebrook. It was a village of moderate size—about two hundred houses being scattered over a tract half a mile square. Occupying a central position was the tavern, a square, two-story building, with a piazza in front, on which was congregated a number of villagers. After rapidly scanning them, the driver said:

"Do you see that tall man over there leanin' against a post?"

"Yes."

"That's your guardeen! That's John Fox himself, as large as life, and just about as homely."

CHAPTER II

THE DANGER SIGNAL

The man pointed out to Harry as his guardian was tall, loosely put together, with a sharp, thin visage surrounded by a thicket of dull-red hair. He came forward as Harry jumped to the ground after descending from the elevated perch, and said: "I reckon this is Harry Vane?"

"That is my name, sir."

"Glad to see you. Just take your traps, and come along with me. Mrs. Fox will have supper ready by the time we come."

Harry was not, on the whole, attracted by the appearance of his guardian. There was a crafty look about the eyes of Mr. Fox which seemed to make his name appropriate. He surveyed his young ward critically.

"You're pretty well grown," he said.

"Yes, sir."

"And look stout and strong."

"I believe I am both."

"My boy, Joel, is as tall as you, but not so hefty. He's goin' to be tall like me. He's a sharp boy—Joel."

"By the way, you didn't write how much property your father left."

"After the funeral bills are paid, I presume there'll be only about three hundred dollars left."

Mr. Fox stopped short and whistled.

"Father hadn't much talent at making money," said Harry, soberly.

"I should say not. Why, that money won't last you no time at all."

"I am old enough to work for a living. Isn't there something I can find to do in Colebrook?"

"I guess I can give you work myself—There's always more or less to do 'round a place. I keep a man part of the time, but I reckon I can let him go and take you on instead. You see, that will count on your board, and you don't want to spend your money too fast."

"Very well, sir. There's only one thing I will stipulate; I will wait a day or two before going to work. I want to look about the place a little."

While this conversation was going on, they had traveled a considerable distance. A little distance ahead appeared a square house, painted yellow, with a barn a little back on the left, and two old wagons alongside.

"That's my house," said John Fox. "There's Joel."

Joel, a tall boy in figure, like his father, came forward and eyed Harry with sharp curiosity.

"How are ye?" said Joel, extending a red hand, covered with warts.

"Pretty well, thank you," said Harry, not much attracted to his new acquaintance.

"Here's Sally, too!" said John Fox. "Sally, this is my ward, Harry Vane."

Sally, who bore a striking family resemblance to her father and brother, giggled.

Mrs. Fox, to whom Harry was introduced at the supper table, was as peculiar in her appearance and as destitute of beauty as the rest of the family.

The next day, Harry, feeling it must be confessed, rather homesick, declined Joel's company, and took an extended stroll about the town. He found that though the railway by which he had come was eight miles distant, there was another, passing within a mile of the village. He struck upon it, and before proceeding far made a startling discovery. There had been some heavy rains, which had washed out the road for a considerable distance, causing the track to give way.

"Good heavens!" thought Harry, "if a train comes over the road before this is mended, there'll be a wreck and loss of life. What can I do?"

Just across the field stood a small house. In the yard the week's washing was hung out. Among the articles was a red tablecloth.

"May I borrow that tablecloth?" asked Harry, in excitement, of a woman in the doorway.

"Land sakes! what for?" she asked.

"To signal the train. The road's washed away."

"Yes, yes; I'm expectin' my darter on that train," answered the woman, now as excited as our hero. "Hurry up! the train's due in fifteen minutes."

Seizing the tablecloth, Harry gathered it quickly into a bundle and ran back to the railroad. He hurried down the track west of a curve which was a few hundred feet beyond the washout, and saw the train coming at full speed. He jumped on a fence skirting the tracks, and waved the tablecloth wildly.

"Will they see it?" he asked himself, anxiously.

It was an anxious moment for Harry as he stood waving the danger signal, uncertain whether it would attract the attention of the engineer. It did! The engineer, though not understanding the meaning of the signal, not knowing indeed, but it might be a boy's freak, prudently heeded it, and reversing the engine, stopped the train a short distance of the place of danger.

"Thank God!" exclaimed Harry, breathing a deep sigh of relief.

The engineer alighted from the train, and when he looked ahead, needed no explanation.

"My boy!" he said, with a shudder, "you have saved the train."

"I am glad of it, sir. My heart was in my mouth, lest you should not see my signal."

By this time the passengers, whose curiosity had been roused by the sudden halt, began to pour out of the cars.

When they saw the washout, strong men turned pale, and ladies grew faint, while many a fervent ejaculation of gratitude was heard at the wonderful escape.

"We owe our lives to this boy!" said the engineer. "It was he who stood on the fence and signaled me. We owe our deliverance to this—tablecloth."

A small man, somewhat portly, pushed his way up to Harry.

"What is your name, my lad?" he asked, brusquely.

"Harry Vane."

"I am the president and leading stockholder of the road, and my property has come very near being the death of me. Gentlemen"—here the president turned to the group of gentlemen around him—"don't you think this boy deserves a testimonial?"

"Yes, yes!" returned the gentlemen, in chorus.

"So do I, and I lead off with a subscription of twenty dollars."

One after another followed the president's lead, the president himself making the rounds bareheaded, and gathering the contributions in his hat.

"Oh, sir!" said Harry, as soon as he understood what was going forward, "don't reward me for what was only my duty. I should be ashamed to accept anything for the little I have done."

"You may count it little to save the lives of a train full of people," said the president, dryly, "but we set a slight value upon our lives and limbs. Are you rich?"

"No, sir."

"So I thought. Well, you needn't be ashamed to accept a little testimonial of our gratitude. You must not refuse."

When all so disposed had contributed, the president gathered the bills from the hat and handed the pile to Harry.

"Take them, my boy," he said, "and make good use of them. I shall owe you a considerable balance, for I value my life at more than twenty dollars. Here is my card. If you ever need a friend, or a service, call on me."

Then the president gave directions to the engineer to run back to the preceding station, where there was a telegraph office, from which messages could be sent in both directions to warn trains of the washout.

Harry was left with his hands full of money, hardly knowing whether he was awake or dreaming.

One thing seemed to him only fair—to give the owner of the tablecloth some small share of the money, as an acknowledgment for the use of her property.

"Here, Madam," said Harry, when he had retraced his steps to the house, "is your tablecloth, for which I am much obliged. It saved the train."

"Well, I'm thankful! Little did I ever think a tablecloth would do so much good. Why, it only cost me a dollar and a quarter."

"Allow me to ask your acceptance of this bill to pay you for the use of it."

"Land sakes! why, you've given me ten dollars!"

"It's all right. It came from the passengers. They gave me something too."

"You didn't tell me your name."

"My name is Harry Vane."

"Do you live round here? I never heerd the name afore."

"I've just come to the village. I'm going to live with John Fox."

"You don't say! Be you any kin to Fox?"

"Not very near. He's my guardian."

"If he hears you've had any money give you, he'll want to take care of it for you."

This consideration had not occurred to Harry. Indeed, he had for so short a time been the possessor of the money, of which he did not know the amount, that this was not surprising.

"Well, good-morning!" he said.

"Good-morning! It's been a lucky mornin' for both of us."

"I must go somewhere where I can count this money unobserved," he said to himself.

Not far away he saw a ruined shed.

Harry entered the shed, and sitting down on a log, took out the bills, which he had hurriedly stuffed in his pocket, and began to count them.

"Almost three hundred dollars!" murmured Harry, joyously. "It has been, indeed, a lucky morning for me. It has nearly doubled my property."

The question arose in his mind: "Should he give this money to Mr. Fox to keep for him?"

"No," he decided, "I won't give him this money. I won't even let him know I have it."

Where, then, could he conceal it? Looking about him, he noticed a little, leather-covered, black trunk, not more than a foot long, and six inches deep. It was locked, but a small key was in the lock.

Opening the trunk he found it empty. The lock seemed in good condition. He made a pile of the bills, and depositing them in this receptacle, locked the trunk and put the key in his pocket.

Now for a place of concealment.

Harry came out of the shed, and looked scrutinizingly around him. Not far away was a sharp elevation surmounted by trees. The hill was a gravelly formation, and therefore dry. At one point near a withered tree, our hero detected a cavity, made either by accident or design. Its location near the tree made it easy to discover.

With a little labor he enlarged and deepened the hole, till he could easily store away the box in its recess, then covered it up carefully, and strewed grass and leaves over all to hide the traces of excavation.

"There that will do," he said, in a tone of satisfaction.

He had reserved for possible need fifteen dollars in small bills, which he put into his pocketbook.

John Fox had heard the news in the post office, and started off at once for the scene of danger.

"How'd they hear of the washout?" he asked, puzzled.

"I heerd that a boy discovered it, and signaled the train," said his neighbor.

"How did he do it?"

"Waved a shawl or somethin'."

"That don't seem likely; where would a boy find a shawl?"

His informant looked puzzled.

"Like as not he borrowed it of Mrs. Brock," he suggested.

Mrs. Brock was the woman living in the small house near by, so that the speaker's surmise was correct. It struck John Fox as possible, and he said so.

"I guess I'll go and ask the Widder Brock," he said. "She must have seen the train, livin' so near as she does."

"I'll go along with you."

The two men soon found themselves on Mrs. Brock's premises.

"Good-mornin,' Mrs. Brock," said John Fox.

"You've come nigh havin' a causality here."

"You're right there, Mr. Fox," answered Mrs. Brock. "I was awful skeered about it, for I thought my Nancy might be on the train. When the boy run into my yard———"

"The boy! What boy?" asked Fox, eagerly.

"It was that boy you are guardeen of."

"What, Harry Vane?" ejaculated Fox, in genuine surprise.

"Tell me all about it, Mrs. Brock."

"Well, you see, he ran into my yard all out of breath, and grabbin' a red tablecloth from the line, asked me if I would lend it to him. 'Land sakes!' says I, 'what do you want of a tablecloth?'"

"'The track's washed away,' he said, 'and I want to signal the train. There's danger of an accident.' Of course, I let him have it, and he did signal the train, standin' on the fence, and wavin' the tablecloth. So the train was saved!"

"And did he bring back the tablecloth?"

"Of course, he did, and that wasn't all. He brought me a ten-dollar bill to pay for the use of it."

"Gave you a ten-dollar bill!" exclaimed John Fox, in amazement. "That was very wrong."

"You hadn't no claim on the money if you are his guardeen. A collection was took up by the passengers, and given to the boy, and he thought I ought to have pay for use of the tablecloth, so he gave me a ten-dollar bill—and a little gentleman he is, too."

"A collection taken up for my ward?" repeated Fox, pricking up his ears. "Well, well! that is news."

John Fox was already on his way back to the road. He was anxious to find his ward.

CHAPTER III

HARRY DISAGREES WITH HIS GUARDIAN

Harry and his guardian met at the dinner table. Mrs. Fox had provided a boiled dinner, to which Harry was ready to do justice.

Mr. Fox seemed unusually pleasant.

"I find, Harry," he said, clearing his throat, "that you have already been distinguishing yourself."

"Then you heard of the narrow escape of the train?" said Harry.

"Yes, I heard that but for your presence of mind, and Mrs. Brock's tablecloth, there would have been a smash-up."

"What on earth are you talkin' about, John Fox?" demanded his wife, curiously.

"Well, you see, Maria, the rain of last night washed away part of the railroad track, and the train would have been plunged into a gully if our young boarder here hadn't seen the danger, and, borrowin' a tablecloth from Mrs. Brock, signaled the train."

"You don't say?"

"That isn't all," resumed John Fox. "The passengers took up a contribution, and I expect gave quite a handsome sum to our young friend."

"How much did the folks give you?" asked Joel eagerly.

"I've got fifteen dollars left," he replied. "I gave some money to Mrs. Brock for the use of the tablecloth."

John Fox looked disappointed and disgusted.

"You don't mean to say," he ejaculated, sharply, "that you gave away almost half of your money for the use of an old tablecloth that would be dear at a dollar?"

"If I hadn't had the tablecloth, I couldn't have attracted the engineer's attention," said Harry, mildly.

There was a little more conversation on the subject, but Harry remained tranquil, and did not appear disturbed by the criticisms elicited by his conduct. He heartily hoped that his guardian's family would not find out how large a sum he had received.

When dinner was over, Harry was about to leave the house, when John Fox said, insinuatingly: "Don't you think you'd better give me that money to keep for you? It will be safer in my hands."

"Thank you, Mr. Fox," said Harry, "but I think I can take care of it myself."

"Fifteen dollars is a good deal of money for a boy like you to carry round with you," said his guardian.

"I don't think I shall lose it, sir," replied the boy.

"Perhaps not, but you will be tempted to spend it wastefully."

John Fox didn't look amiable. He was in doubt whether he might not properly take from his ward the money by force, but it occurred to him that it would be better not to assert his authority quite so soon.

"We will speak of this again," he said.

"It is well I didn't bring all the money home. I wonder how soon Mr. Fox will make another attempt to secure the sum I have with me," thought Harry.

The attempt was made that same night.

Harry was afraid he would be expected to occupy the same room with Joel, in which case he could hope for no privacy, and would be unable to conceal his money, which he had little doubt his guardian intended to secure, either by fair means or foul. It chanced, however, that Joel slept in a small bedroom opening out of his parents' chamber. So Harry was assigned an attic room, in the end of the house, the sides sloping down to the eaves. It was inferior to the chambers on the second floor, but our hero was not disposed to complain. He valued solitude more than superior finish.

Harry's suspicion was roused by the circumstance that his guardian did not again refer to his money, nor did he manifest any disappointment at his ward's declining to intrust him with it.

During the evening, Joel brought out a backgammon board, and proposed to Harry to play. If there would have been anything to read Harry would have preferred entertaining himself in that way, but Mr. Fox didn't appear to be literary. There were a few books in the house, but they were not of an attractive character.

Partly in backgammon, partly in conversation with the son and heir of the Foxes, the time passed till half-past eight o'clock.

"Joel, you can go to bed," said his mother. "It is half-past eight."

Joel yawned, and interposed no objection.

"You may as well go, too, Harry," said Mrs. Fox.

"I am ready to go to bed," said Harry.

In fact, he felt rather sleepy, and anticipated little pleasure in sitting up in the far from exciting company of Mr. and Mrs. Fox.

"Joel!" said his mother, "take this candle and show Harry upstairs in the attic chamber."

"Yes, mam."

So, preceded by Joel, Harry went up two flights of stairs to the attic room reserved for him. It was the only room that had been finished off, and the garret outside looked dark and forbidding.

"I would be scared to sleep up here," said his companion.

"I shall not be at all frightened, Joel," said Harry.

"Good-night. Just hold the candle while I go downstairs."

When he was fairly all alone, Harry began to look about him, to ascertain in what kind of quarters he was to pass the night. To begin with he examined the door, he ascertained that it was a common latch door, and there was no lock. There was nothing to prevent anyone entering the room during the night. There was a small cot bed in one corner, a chair, and an old wooden chest. There was no bureau nor washstand. The absence of the latter annoyed Harry.

He learned afterward that he was expected to go downstairs and wash in a large basin in the kitchen sink—wiping his face on a brown, roll towel which was used by the entire family. This was quite unsatisfactory to Harry, who was scrupulously neat in his tastes.

"This isn't a palace exactly," Harry said to himself.

Then came the thought, "What was he to do with his money?"

Now, it so happened that Harry was the possessor of two pocketbooks—one—shabby, and well worn, which he had failed to throw away on buying another just before he left home. In connection with this, a scheme for outwitting Mr. Fox came into his mind. He folded up a fragment of newspaper, and put it into the old pocketbook, bulging it out till it looked well filled, and this he left in the pocket of his pantaloons.

"Now to hide the other," said he to himself.

He looked about the room seeking for some place of concealment. Finally he noticed in one portion of the floor a square board, which looked as if it might be lifted. He stooped over and succeeded in raising it. The space beneath was about a foot in depth—the lower level being the lathing and plastering of the room below.

"That will do," said Harry, in a tone of satisfaction. "I don't think Mr. Fox will find my money here," and dropping the pocketbook into the cavity he replaced the square board. Then he went to bed and awaited results.

When Harry had gone up to his bed, Mr. and Mrs. Fox naturally began to compare notes respecting him.

"That new boy rides a high horse," said Mrs. Fox, grimly. "Are you going to allow it?"

"Certainly not."

"He wouldn't give up his money to you, though you are his guardeen."

"Very true, but I mean to have it all the same. I shall go up to his bedroom after he is asleep, and then it will be the easiest thing in the world to take the pocketbook without his knowin' anything about it."

"He'll know it in the mornin'."

"Let him! Possession is nine p'ints of the law, Mrs. Fox."

"He might say you stole it."

"He can't do that, for I'm his guardeen, don't you see?"

A little after ten Mr. Fox, considering that Harry must be sound asleep, decided to make him a visit. He removed his shoes, and in his stocking feet, candle in hand, began to ascend the narrow and steep staircase which led to the attic.

"Shall I go with you, John?" queried his helpmeet.

"No, I guess I can manage alone."

His wife wanted to share in the excitement of the night visit. There was something alluring in the thought of creeping upstairs, and removing by stealth, the pocketbook of the new inmate of their home.

Left to himself, Mr. Fox pursued his way up the attic stairs. They creaked a little under his weight, and, much to his annoyance, when he reached the landing at the top he coughed.

"I hope the boy won't hear me," he said to himself.

He paused an instant, then softly opened the door of Harry's chamber.

All seemed satisfactory. Our hero was lying quietly in bed, apparently in a peaceful sleep. Ordinarily he would have been fast asleep by this time, but the expectation of a visit from his guardian had kept him awake beyond his usual time. He had heard Mr. Fox cough, and so, even before the door opened, he had warning of the visit.

Harry was not a nervous boy, and had such command of himself, that, even when Mr. Fox bent over, and, by the light of the candle, examined his face, he never stirred nor winked, though he very much wanted to laugh.

"All is safe! The boy is sound asleep," whispered Mr. Fox to himself.

He set the candle on the floor, and then taking up Harry's pantaloons, thrust his hand into the pocket.

The very first pocket contained the pocketbook which our hero had put there. Mr. Fox would have opened and examined the contents on the spot, but he heard a cough from the bed, and, quickly put the pocketbook into his own pocket, apprehending that his ward might wake up, and taking up the candle, noiselessly withdrew from the chamber.

After he had fairly gone, Harry had a quiet laugh to himself.

Mr. Fox returned in triumph to his own chamber, where his wife was anxiously waiting for him.

"Have you got it, Mr. F.," she asked, eagerly.

"Got it? Why shouldn't I get it?"

"Well, open it, and let us see what it contains."

This Mr. Fox proceeded to do. But no sooner did his glance rest on its contents than his lower jaw fell, and his eyes opened wide in perplexity.

"Well, what are you staring at like a fool?" demanded his wife, who was not so situated that she could see the contents of the pocketbook.

"Look at this, Mrs. F.," said her husband, in a hollow voice. "There's no money here—only this piece of newspaper."

"Well, well, of all the fools I ever saw you are about the most stupid!" ejaculated Mrs. Fox. "What you undertake you generally carry through, do you? After all the fuss you've brought down a pocketbook stuffed with waste paper."

"I don't understand it," said Fox, his face assuming a look of perplexity. "Surely the boy told the truth when he said he had fifteen dollars."

"Of course! Joel saw the money—a roll of bills, and saw him take them out of his pocketbook. He must have taken them out. Did you search all his pockets?"

"No; when I found the pocketbook I thought I was all right."

"Just like a man!" retorted Mrs. Fox. "I'll go up myself, and see if I can't manage better than you."

"Then you'd better take this wallet, and put it back in his pocket."

"Give it to me, then."

With a firm step Mrs. Fox took the candle, and took her turn in going up the attic stairs.

CHAPTER IV

MRS. FOX COMES TO GRIEF

Harry confidently anticipated a second visit to his chamber.

He was rather surprised when the door was again opened, and Mrs. Fox entered. Opening his eyes a little way, he saw her, after a brief glance at the bed, go to the chair containing his pantaloons, and put back the deceptive wallet. She was about to prosecute a further search, when Harry decided that matters had gone far enough. He did not fancy their night visits, and meant to stop them if he could.

Chance favored his design. A puff of air from the door, which Mrs. Fox had left wide open, extinguished the candle, and left the room, as there was no moon, in profound darkness.

"Drat the candle!" he heard Mrs. Fox say.

Then a mischievous idea came to Harry. In his native village lived a man who had passed a considerable time in the wild region beyond the Missouri River, and had mingled familiarly with the Indians. From him Harry had learned how to imitate the Indian warwhoop.

"I'll scare the old lady," thought Harry, smiling to himself.

Immediately there rang out from the bed, in the darkness and silence, a terrific warwhoop, given in Harry's most effective style.

Mrs. Fox was not a nervous woman ordinarily, but she was undeniably frightened at the unexpected sound.

"Heavens and earth, what's that?" she ejaculated, and dropping our hero's clothes, retreated in disorder, almost stumbling downstairs in her precipitate flight. Dashing into the chamber where Mr. Fox was waiting for her, she sank into a chair, gasping for breath.

"Good gracious, Maria, what's the matter?" exclaimed her husband, gazing at her in astonishment.

"I—don't—know," she gasped.

"You look as if you had seen a ghost."

"I haven't seen anything," said his wife, recovering her breath, "but I've heard something terrible. It's my belief the attic is haunted. I went upstairs and put back the wallet, and was looking to see if I could find another, when all at once the candle went out, and a terrible noise shook the chamber."

"What was it like, Mrs. F.?"

"I can't tell you. I never heard anything like it before. All I know is, I wouldn't go up there again tonight for anything."

"Did the boy sleep through it all?"

"How can I tell? The candle was out."

"Perhaps he blew it out."

"Perhaps you're a fool Mr. Fox. It wasn't near the bed, and he was fast asleep, for I looked at him. It made me think of—of Peter," and Mrs. Fox shuddered.

Peter had been taken from the poorhouse three years ago by Mr. Fox, and apprenticed to him by the town authorities. According to popular report he had been cruelly treated and insufficiently fed, until he was taken sick and had died in the very bedroom where Mrs. Fox had been so frightened. This may explain how it was that a woman so strong-minded had had her nerves so easily upset.

"We won't talk of Peter," said Mr. Fox, shortly, for to him, also, the subject was an unpleasant one. "I suppose you didn't find another wallet?"

"No, I didn't. You can order the boy to give it up to-morrow. The best thing to do now is to go to bed and rest."

The breakfast hour at the house of Mr. Fox was half past six. Harry was called at six, and was punctual at the table. Mr. Fox cast a suspicious glance at his ward, but the boy looked so perfectly unconcerned, that he acquitted him of any knowledge of the night visit.

"How did you sleep, Harry?" asked Mrs. Fox.

"Soundly, thank you," answered Harry, politely.

"You didn't hear any—strange noises, then?"

"No."

"Now, Harry," said Mr. Fox, after breakfast, "we may as well speak of our future arrangements. I have considerable to do on my twenty acres of land, and I can give you work here."

"What compensation do you offer, sir?"

"As a boarder I should have to charge you five dollars a week for your board, and fifty cents extra for your washing—that would go to Mrs. Fox; as well as pay twenty-five cents a week for your mending. That also would go to my wife. Now, if you work for me, I will take off three dollars, making the charge to you only two dollars and seventy-five cents per week."

"Don't you think, Mr. Fox, that is rather low pay for my services?"

"I might say two dollars and a quarter," said Mr. Fox, deliberating.

Harry smiled to himself. He had not the slightest idea of working for any such trifle, but he did not care to announce his determination yet.

"I will pay full price for a week, Mr. Fox," he said, "and during that time I will consider your offer."

"I may not offer you as favorable terms a week from now," said Fox, who wanted to get his ward to work at once.

"I will take my chance of it, sir. I prefer to have a few days of freedom."

"By the way, Harry, don't you think you had better give me your money to keep? You might lose it."

"You are very kind, Mr. Fox; but I am not afraid of losing it."

After breakfast Harry went to walk. His steps naturally tended to the place where he had left the greater part of his treasure. It was possible that he had been seen hiding it, and he thought on the whole it would be better to find another place of concealment.

"Joel," said his mother, "follow Harry, and see where he goes. He may be goin' to hide his money. But don't let him see you."

"All right, mam; I'll do it. I wish I had followed him yesterday."

A position as detective would have suited Joel. Whatever was secret or stealthy had a charm for him.

In the present instance he managed to shadow Harry very successfully. The task was made easier, because our hero had no idea that anyone was following him.

"So he's goin' to the railroad," said Joel, to himself

Arrived at the railroad track, Harry's course diverged to the hillock, at the top of which he had concealed his treasure.

Joel posted himself at a point where he had a good view of the elevation, and could see what Harry was doing. He saw our hero digging at a particular spot, and concluded that he was going to hide the fifteen dollars there. What was his surprise and delight when he saw him dig up and expose to view a large roll of bills.

"Oh, cracky!" ejaculated Joel, "there must be a hundred dollars in that roll of bills. Wouldn't dad open his eyes if he saw it?"

Unconscious of observation, Harry held the money in his hand and deliberated. Then he put it in his pocket, resolved to think over at his leisure its ultimate place of deposit.

Now, unfortunately for Joel, just at this moment he slipped from his perch on the branch of a small tree, and for about half a minute what Harry did was concealed from him. He clambered into the tree again, but only to see Harry filling up the hole again.

He didn't want Harry to catch sight of him when he descended from the hill, and accordingly scuttled away sufficiently far to escape suspicion, yet not too far to entirely lose sight of Harry's movements.

Five minutes later Harry descended from the hill, and bent his steps toward that part of the railway where the accident had occurred. Joel, who had hastened away in a different direction, went back to the hill as soon as he thought it would be safe, and eagerly ascended it. He found without difficulty the spot where Harry had been digging. With the help of a fragment of wood which he had picked up below, he in turn began to dig—his eyes glistening with expectation and cupidity.

He kept digging, but gradually became anxious, as the expected treasure did not show itself.

"I'm sure I have dug deep enough," he said to himself.

"He must have took the money when I fell from the tree," thought Joel, crestfallen. "He's served me a mean trick. Won't I tell dad, though, and get him into trouble? Oh, no!"

Meanwhile Harry, not knowing how narrowly he had escaped being robbed, pursued his way to the railway.

"If I were only in my old home," he thought, "I would ask Mr. Howard to take care of it for me. Then I should know it was all right."

He thought of the president of the railroad, to whom he was principally indebted for the money.

"If I could only see him," he thought, "I would ask him to take care of it for me."

What was his surprise, when, on reaching the depot, the first person on whom his eyes fell was the very gentleman of whom he was thinking.

"How do you do, sir?" said Harry, politely.

"Ah, my young friend that saved the train!" said the president cordially. "I hope you haven't spent the money you received on riotous living."

"No. Will you take care of it for me? I don't want to spend it, and I am afraid of losing it."

"Well, my boy, if you really desire it, I will take the money."

"I shall regard it as a very great favor."

No sooner said than done. They went into the depot and Harry, counting out two hundred and fifty dollars, passed it over to the president.

He made out a brief receipt, signing it, "Thomas Conway, President of the Craven County Railroad," and Harry pocketed it with a feeling of relief.

While he was standing in front of the depot waiting for the arrival of the eight-thirty train, Joel came up.

"Goin' a-travelin'?" asked Joel, with a grin.

"Not this morning."

"I wish I had a hundred dollars!" continued Joel, surveying Harry sharply. "I'd make a journey out West. Say, Harry, did you ever have a hundred dollars in your pocket?"

"Yes."

"Maybe you've got it now?"

"Where should I get it?" demanded Harry.

"I do'no. Jest empty your pockets, and le'me see how much you've got."

"Thank you; I don't see any use in it," said Harry.

"You dassent!"

"Very well! Call it that."

"Joel's been spying on me. He must have seen me on the hill," concluded Harry. "It's well I gave most of my money to Mr. Conway."

CHAPTER V

MR. FOX LEARNS HARRY'S SECRET

Harry had acted none too soon. It happened that his secret had been discovered not only by Joel, but by Joel's father, that very morning.

About ten o'clock Mr. Fox had occasion to go to the village. In the post office he met an acquaintance from a neighboring town, with whom he passed the usual compliments.

"By the way, Fox," said his friend, "I had a narrow escape the other day."

"What was it, Pearson?"

"Came near being smashed up on the railroad. There would have been an end to us, but for a brave boy, who signaled the train in time."

"That boy was my ward," said John Fox, complacently.

"You don't say so! Well, he was a lucky chap."

"I don't think so. He didn't get much for his bravery."

"I don't see how you can say that. How much money did he get?"

"Twenty-five dollars, and of that he gave ten to the woman whose tablecloth he borrowed."

"There's some mistake about that. There must have been forty or fifty bills put into his hands."

"Is this true?" ejaculated Fox, in amazement.

"Just as true as I'm standing here. If there wasn't two or three hundred dollars I'll eat my head."

"The artful young rascal!" exclaimed Fox, in virtuous indignation.

"Perhaps he thought you would take it from him. The boy was smart," said Pearson, laughing.

"You call it smart! I call it base and treacherous!"

Mr. Fox walked thoughtfully away. He was considering how he should get hold of his ward's money. It was not a question easy to answer. Evidently Harry was a boy who kept his own counsel, and knew how to take care of himself.

"Joel seems to have a great partiality for my society," thought Harry, when, after dinner, his guardian's son continued to follow him about.

Our hero would have been quite willing to dispense with Joel's companionship, but, being good-natured, he did not feel like dismissing him, as he would have done had he suspected that the boy was acting as a spy upon him, at his father's request.

Mr. Fox said very little to his ward at the table, but Harry felt that he was eyeing him intently.

After supper Harry was about to leave the room when Mr. Fox stopped him.

"Wait a moment, young man," he said, in a commanding tone.

"Very well, sir," returned Harry, quietly.

"How much money did the passengers give you?"

"Almost three hundred dollars," answered Harry, composedly.

"Did you ever hear the like?" exclaimed Mrs. Fox, in amazement. "If it had only been Joel."

"Thunder!" exclaimed that young gentleman. "Well, you was lucky. No such luck for me!"

"It is well you have told me," said John Fox; "not but I knew before. I met one of the passengers to-day, and he gave me an idea how much it was. You will please hand it over to me, and I will take care of it."

"I shall not be able to comply with your request, Mr. Fox," said Harry. "I have not the money with me."

"I don't believe it. You had it this morning. And Joel has been with you ever since; so you haven't had time to hide it."

"So that was the reason you favored me with your company, Joel," said Harry, with a glance at his guardian's son.

"All you've got to do is to hand over that money now, Harry Vane. Mind, I intend to have it."

"I assure you, Mr. Fox, that I haven't the money with me."

"Where is it, then?" asked Mr. Fox, incredulous.

"I have put it into the hands of a gentleman in whom I have confidence, who will take care of it for me."

"What's the man's name?" demanded John Fox.

"That is my secret."

"You have rebelled against my lawful authority. Maria, what is it my duty to do with this boy?"

"Lock him up!" answered Mrs. Fox, grimly.

"A good suggestion, Mrs. F. Imprisonment may change the boy's ideas. He may repent his base conduct."

"Now, young man," said Fox, in a tone of authority, "go up to your chamber, and stay there till you're ready to obey orders."

Harry hesitated a moment, then quietly went upstairs. Mr. Fox was relieved, for he was a little apprehensive that his ward would prove rebellious and decline to obey.

John Fox stole up after his ward, and Harry heard the door bolted on the outside.

He was a prisoner.

When he heard the bolt slide in the lock, he said to himself: "Mr. Fox and I can never agree. He has not yet been appointed my guardian, and he never will receive the appointment. I have the right to choose for myself, as Mr. Howard told me, and I mean to exercise it."

Some of my readers may, perhaps, picture Harry as forcing open the door of his chamber and rushing from the house, breathing loud defiance as he went. But he was a sensible boy, and meditated nothing of the kind.

"I can wait till morning," he reflected. "I don't think I shall be here twenty hours hence, but I mean to get a good night's sleep. It will be time enough to decide in the morning what I will do."

So, in spite of his imprisonment, Harry enjoyed a comfortable night's sleep, and was awakened in the morning by hearing his door opened.

Mr. Fox entered, and sat down on a chair by the bed.

"Good-morning, sir," said Harry, composedly.

"What I want to know is, have you made up your mind to do as I told you last night?"

"I prefer to keep it in my possession."

"I guess I'll have to keep you here a little longer."

"Then be kind enough to send me up some breakfast. I am paying my board. I shall object to paying unless I get my meals regularly."

This consideration weighed with John Fox, and he sent Joel up with a cup of coffee and some dry bread, five minutes later.

"By the way, Joel, come up here about the middle of the forenoon; I want to say a few words to you in private."

"All right, I'll come. I must go downstairs now."

"I wonder what he wants to see me about?" said Joel, to himself.

Joel made a pretty shrewd guess, and resolved, by all means, to keep the appointment.

He was anxious to get his father out of the way, but John Fox was unusually deliberate in his motions. Finally, about half-past nine, he left the house for the village.

Presently his mother said: "Joel, if you'll stay and mind the house, I'll run over to Mrs. Bean's and borrow some sugar."

His mother put on her bonnet, and started across a field to her nearest neighbor's.

"Now's my time," thought Joel. "Mam's sure to get talkin' with Mrs. Bean and stay half an hour or more."

He ran up the garret stairs, and drew the bolt that held Harry captive.

"Joel, I want you to let me out of this place."

"Oh, gracious!" exclaimed Joel, in apparent dismay. "Dad would give me the wu'st kind of a lickin'."

"Would he know how I got out?" asked Harry.

"I don't know. What are you willing to give?"

Harry saw that it was merely a matter of bargaining, and finally prevailed upon Joel to release him for a five-dollar bill.

"I want the money now," said Joel.

"How do I know that you will do as you have agreed?"

"Give me the money, and I'll tell you."

Harry passed over the bank bill, and Joel said:

"Dad's gone to the village, and mam's gone over to Mrs. Bean's. All you've got to do is to go downstairs, and walk out."

Harry was by no means slow to take the hint.

"Good-by, Joel," he said, extending his hand; "I won't forget the favor you've done me."

"I don't know what dad'll say. There'll be an awful fuss. Just give me a box on the ear, won't you?"

"What for?"

"I'll tell dad you gave me an awful clip on the side of the head, and ran off, though I tried to stop you."

"All right," said Harry, laughing.

He gave Joel the required box on the ear, tripped him up, laying him gently on his back on the landing, and then, with a friendly "good-by," he ran down the stairs, and before Mrs. Fox returned from her call was a mile away.

She found Joel wiping his eyes.

"What's the matter, Joel?" she asked.

"That boy, Harry, called me upstairs, and got me to open the door. Then he gave me an almighty clip on the side of my head that almost stunned me, then he knocked me over, and ran out of the house as fast as he could run—my head aches awful!"

"The owdacious young ruffian!" ejaculated Mrs. Fox. "To beat my poor, dear Joel so! Never mind. Joel, dear, I'll give you a piece of pie and some cake. As for that boy, he'll be hung some day, I reckon!"

After eating the cake and pie, which were luxuries in that frugal household, Joel said he felt better. He went out behind the house, and taking out the five-dollar note, surveyed it with great satisfaction.

CHAPTER VI

AN EXCITING CHASE

When John Fox went to the village he usually stopped first at the tavern, and invested ten cents in a glass of whisky. Here he met two or three of his cronies.

"Folks say you've got a new boarder, Fox," said Bill Latimer, as he laid down his glass on the counter.

"Yes," answered Fox, complacently. "I'm his guardeen."

"Folks say he got a pile of money for saving the train."

"He got a pretty stiff sum," answered Fox cautiously.

"Do you keep his money?"

"Yes."

"Is he easy to manage?" asked John Blake.

"Well, some folks might find trouble with him," said Fox, complacently. "The fact is, gentlemen, I don't mind telling you that he's been trying to buck agin' his guardeen a'ready. Where do you think I left him?" continued Fox, chuckling.

"Where?"

"Up in the attic, locked up in his chamber. I'm goin' to feed him on bread and water a while, just to show him what sort of a man John Fox is."

A grin overspread the face of Eben Bond, who had just looked out of the front window.

"So you left him in the attic, hey?" he said, waggishly.

"Yes, I did. Do you mean to say I didn't?"

"I'm willin' to bet he isn't there now."

"You just tell me what you mean, Eben Bond!" said John Fox, provoked.

"I mean that I saw that boy of yours go by the tavern only two minutes since."

"Where did he go? In what direction?" demanded Fox, eagerly.

"Down toward the river."

"He's running away," Fox said to himself, in dismay. "How in the the world did he get out?"

He ran up the road, gazing anxiously on this side and on that, hoping to come upon the runaway. One thing was favorable; it was a straight road, with no roads opening out of it at least a mile beyond the tavern. It led by the river at a point half a mile on.

"I'll catch him yet. He can't escape me!" Fox reflected.

John Fox pushed on breathless, and a minute later came in sight of the fugitive.

Harry had sobered down to a walk, thinking himself no longer in danger. If Mr. Fox had been wise enough to keep silent till he had come within a few rods he might have caught him easily, but excitement and anger were too much for prudence, and he called out, angrily: "Just wait till I get hold of you, you young villain! I'll give you a lesson."

Harry turned quickly and saw his enemy close upon him.

That was enough. He set out on what the boys call a dead run, though he hardly knew in what direction to look for refuge. But through the trees at the west side of the road he caught sight of something that put new hope into his heart. It was a boat, floating within three feet of shore. In it sat a boy of about Harry's own age. It was Willie Foster.

There was no time for ceremony, Harry sprang into the boat, and, seizing an idle oar, pushed out into the river.

The owner of the boat, who had been thoughtfully gazing into the water, looked up in surprise.

"Well, that's cool!" he ejaculated.

"I beg your pardon," said Harry, still plying the oar; "I couldn't help it; Mr. Fox is after me."

John Fox, by this time, stood on the river bank shaking his fist, with a discomfited expression, at his intended victim.

"Come back here!" he shouted.

"Thank you, I would rather not," answered Harry, still increasing the distance between himself and his guardian.

"You Willie Foster, row the boat back!" bawled John Fox,

"Is your name Willie Foster?" asked Harry, turning to his companion, who was looking, with a puzzled expression, from one to the other.

"Yes."

"Then, Willie, if you will help me row over to the other side of the river and set me off there, I'll give you a dollar."

"I'll do it," said Willie, seizing the other oar, "but you needn't give me any money."

To his intense disgust, Fox saw the boat, propelled by the two boys, leaping forward energetically, while he stood helplessly on the bank.

The other bank was half a mile away, and could not be reached except by a bridge a considerable distance away. The two boys said little until the trip was accomplished.

"I hope you won't get into any serious trouble with Mr. Fox," said Harry, as they drew near the bank.

"I don't care for old Fox, and father doesn't like him, either."

As he got out of the boat he pressed a dollar into Willie's reluctant hand.

"Now, which way had I better go?"

"Take that footpath. It will lead to Medfield. There you can take the cars."

"Good-by, Willie; and thank you."

Willie didn't row back immediately. John Fox was lying in wait on the other side, and he didn't care to meet him.

Harry pushed on till he reached a highway. He felt in doubt as to where it might lead him, but followed it at a venture. He wondered whether John Fox would pursue him, and from time to time looked back to make sure that his guardian was not on his trail. In about three hours he found himself eight miles away. Then, for the first time, he felt that it might be safe to stop and rest. In a village a little way back he had entered a bakeshop and purchased some rolls and a glass of milk, which he ate with a good relish.

He resumed his walk, but had not gone a quarter of a mile when he heard the noise of wheels, which on coming up with him, came to a halt.

"Shall I give you a lift?" said the driver of the team.

Looking up, he saw that it was a covered wagon with four wheels, such as is often to be met in New England towns. The man who held the reins was of large frame and portly, with dark hair and whiskers. He might be about forty-five years of age.

"Thank you, sir, said Harry.

"Where are you bound, if you don't mind my being inquisitive?"

"I don't know," answered Harry, doubtfully. "I'm seeking my fortune, as they say."

"Well you ought to find it," returned the other, after a deliberate survey of his young companion. "You're well-built, and look healthy and strong. Have you got any money?"

"A little. My father died lately and left me three hundred dollars. He recommended to me as guardian a man named John Fox, living eight miles back. Well, I have tried Mr. Fox, and I prefer to be my own guardian."

"I've heard of John Fox. He's fox by name and fox by nature. So you and he didn't hitch horses. When did you leave him?"

"This morning. I don't know but I may say that I am running away from him, as I left without his knowledge or permission, but as he is not yet my legal guardian, I don't consider that he has any right to interfere with me."

"You haven't told me your name yet."

"My name is Harry Vane."

"I am the Magician of Madagascar. You may have heard of me."

"I don't think I have," said Harry, puzzled.

"I have been before the public many years," he said. "I give magical entertainments, and, in the course of the last twenty years, have traveled all over the continent."

"You see," explained Harry, apologetically, "I have always lived in a small country town, where there were few amusements, and so I know very little of such things. I never saw a magical entertainment in my life."

"Didn't you, indeed? Then you shall see me perform to-night. I am to give a magical soiree in Conway, the town we are coming to."

"I should like it very much, Mr. ——" and Harry paused in doubt.

"I am called Professor Hemenway—Hiram Hemenway," said the magician.

"Do you like your business?" asked Harry, curiously.

"Why shouldn't I? I have a chance to travel. The people appreciate my efforts and reward me generously."

By a fortunate accident Harry happened to turn in his seat and look through a small window in the back part of the wagon. What he saw startled him. In a buggy, ten rods back, he recognized his late guardian and Joel. They were making good speed, and were doubtless in pursuit of him.

Harry quickly imparted his discovery to his companion.

"Don't let them capture me!" he said.

"I should like to see him do it," responded the professor. "Get into the back part of the wagon, and crouch down."

Harry did as directed.

Then the professor slackened his speed, and allowed the pursuers to overtake him.

"I say, stranger," said Fox, as he drew up alongside. "A boy ran away from me this morning. Perhaps you have seen him?"

"I saw a boy about a mile back," said the magician, reflectively, "a stout, good-looking lad, dark-brown hair, and a pleasant expression; didn't look at all like you. I chatted with him a while. He said he was leaving a man who claimed to be his guardian, but wasn't."

"The young liar!" ejaculated Fox, wrathfully. "Where is he now?"

"Is he in your wagon?" put in Joel, sharply.

"If he were you'd see him, wouldn't you?"

"In behind you?"

"Yes, are you kidnapping him?" demanded Fox, fiercely.

"There is a boy in the back part of my wagon," said the magician, coolly. "If you ain't afraid of smallpox, you may see him. Which shall it be, you or the boy?"

A pallid hue overspread the face of John Fox, which was increased by an agonizing moan, which appeared to proceed from behind the magician.

"Turn the horse, Joel," was all he said.

He whipped up his horse without a word, and did not pull up for half a mile.

"You can come out now, Harry," said the professor, with a queer smile. "I am a ventriloquist, and that moan did the business."

CHAPTER VII

A NEW ENGAGEMENT

Harry was not a little relieved at his narrow escape. He did not propose to be taken captive without making a strong resistance; but still, in a struggle with Mr. Fox and Joel, he felt that he would be considerably at a disadvantage.

"I am much obliged to you for saving me, Professor Hemenway," he said.

"You are quite welcome. So you didn't like old Fox?"

"Not much."

"He doesn't appear to like you any better."

"There isn't much love lost between us," returned Harry, laughing.

"How do you like the boy?"

"He served me a good turn—for five dollars—but he would help capture me for the same money, or less."

"You seem to know him."

"He is fond of money, and would do almost anything for it."

"You thank me for saving you from capture, my lad," continued the magician. "Well, I had an object in it—a selfish object."

Harry looked puzzled.

"It struck me that I needed a boy about your size, and character, for a general assistant, to sell tickets, take money, and help me on the stage. How do you like the idea?"

"I like it," answered Harry; "but there is one objection."

"What is that?"

"I don't come from Madagascar," responded Harry, slyly.

Professor Hemenway laughed.

"You've been as near there as I have," he said. "Did you really think I came from Madagascar?"

"You look more as if you came from Maine, sir."

"You've hit it! There's where I did come from. I was raised twenty-five miles from Portland on a farm. But it would never do to put that on the bills. People are ready to pay more for imported than for native curiosities. However, to come to business. I had a young man traveling with me who wasn't suited to the business. He was a dry-goods clerk when I took him, and is better adapted to that business than to mine. He left me last week, and I have been in a quandary about his successor. How much do you consider your time worth?"

"Just at present it isn't worth much. If you will pay my traveling expenses, that will satisfy me."

"I will do better than that I will give you five dollars a week besides, if business is good."

"Thank you, sir. I think I shall enjoy traveling."

There are few boys who do not like change of scene, and the chance of seeing new places is attractive to all. Harry was decidedly of the opinion that he had a streak of luck. It would be much better in all ways than living with his late guardian, and working for partial board.

As they approached the village of Conway, Harry's attention was drawn to a variety of posters setting forth, in mammoth letters, that the world-renowned Magician of Madagascar would give a magical soiree at the Town Hall in the evening. Tickets, fifteen cents; children under twelve years, ten cents. The posters, furthermore, attracted attention by a large figure of the professor, dressed in bizarre style, performing one of his tricks.

"That draws attention," observed the professor, "particularly among the boys. I think I shall have a hall full this evening. An audience of three hundred will pay very well. My expenses are light. I do most of my traveling in this wagon, and at hotels I get the usual professional reduction."

"Did it take you long to learn the business?"

"I have been learning all along. Every now and then I add a new trick. I will teach you some."

"I might leave you and set up on my own hook when I have learned," suggested Harry, with a smile.

"It will be some time before you look old enough for a magician. When you are, I'll give you my blessing and send you out."

Meanwhile they had been jogging along, and were already in the main street of Conway. The professor drew up in front of the village hotel, and a groom came forward and took his horse.

"Wait a minute my friend," said the professor. "Harry, you can help me take my implements out of the back of the wagon."

These "implements" were of a heterogeneous character, but all would come in use in the evening. A number of boys watched their transfer with mingled awe and curiosity.

"What's them?" Harry heard one ask another, in a half-whispered tone.

"Those," said the professor, in an impressive tone, turning toward the boys. "Those are paraphernalia!"

The boys looked more awestruck than ever. All inwardly resolved to go to the Town Hall that evening, and get a nearer view of the articles which had such a grand name.

After a while Harry came downstairs from the room assigned him, and stood on the piazza. One of the boys drew near him cautiously.

"Are you the magician's son?" he asked.
"No," answered Harry, smiling.
"Do you come from Madagascar?"
"I have not been there recently."
"Are all the people there magicians?"
"Not quite all."
This information was rather scanty, but it was whispered about among the boys, the first boy boasting that he had a talk with the young man magician. If Harry had heard himself called thus, he would have been very much amused.
Directly after supper Harry went with his employer to assist in preparing the stage for the evening performance. Though novice, he acquitted himself to the satisfaction of his employer, who congratulated himself on having secured so efficient an assistant. Half an hour before the performance he stationed himself in the entry, provided with tickets. He sat at a small table, and received the crowd. Though new to the business, he managed to make change rapidly. He found his position one in which he had a chance to study human nature. During the evening Harry was called upon to assist the professor in some of his tricks. Some boys would have been embarrassed upon finding themselves objects of general attention, but Harry was by temperament cool and self-possessed. He had been fond of declamation at school, and this had accustomed him, to some extent, to a public appearance.
The entertainment was in two parts, with an intermission of ten minutes.
"I wish you were a singer," said the professor, when they were standing behind the screen.
"Why?" asked Harry.
"Because the audience sometimes gets impatient during the intermission. If I could put you on for a song, it would help quiet them."
"I can sing a little," said Harry, modestly.
"What can you sing?"
"How would 'The Last Rose of Summer' do?"
"Capital. Can you sing it?"
"I can try."
"You are sure you won't break down? That would make a bad impression."
"I can promise you I won't break down, sir."
"Then I'll give you a trial. Are you ready to appear at once?"
"Yes, sir."
"Wait, then, till I announce you."
The professor came from behind the screen, and, addressing the audience, said: "Ladies and gentlemen, lest you should find the necessary intermission tedious, I am happy to announce to you that the young vocalist, Master Harry Vane, has kindly consented to favor you with one of his popular melodies. He has selected by request, 'The Last Rose of Summer.'"
Harry could hardly refrain from laughing when he heard this introduction.
"One would think I was a well-known singer," he said to himself.
He came forward, and, standing before the audience, with his face a little flushed, made a graceful bow. Then, pausing an instant, he commenced the song announced. He had not sung two lines before the professor, who waited the result with some curiosity and some anxiety, found that he could sing. His voice was high, clear, and musical, and his rendition was absolutely correct. The fact was, Harry had taken lessons in a singing school at home, and had practiced privately also, so that he had reason to feel confidence in himself.
The song was listened to with earnest attention and evident enjoyment by all. When the last strain died away, and Harry made his farewell bow, there was an enthusiastic burst of applause, emphasized by the clapping of hands and the stamping of feet.
"You did yourself proud, my boy!" said the gratified Professor. "They want you on again."
This seemed evident from the noise.

"Can't you sing something else?"

"Very well, sir."

Harry was certainly pleased with this evidence of popular favor. He had never before sung a solo before an audience, and, although he had felt that he could, he was glad to find that he had not overestimated his powers.

Once more he stood before the audience.

"I thank you for your kindness," he said. "I will now sing you a comic song."

He sang a song very popular at that time, the words and air of which were familiar to all. While it did not afford him so good a chance to show his musical capacity, it was received with much greater favor than the first song.

There was a perfect whirlwind of applause, and a third song was called for.

"I would rather not sing again, professor," said Harry.

"You needn't. They would keep you singing all the evening if you would allow it. Better leave off when they are unsatisfied."

"Ladies and gentlemen," he said, "Master Vane thanks you for your kind applause, but he makes it an unvarying rule never to sing but two songs in an evening. He never broke that rule but once, and that was at the special request of the governor-general of Canada. I shall now have the pleasure of performing for your amusement, one of my most popular experiments."

"Well, you have pleased the people, and that is the main point. By Jove! my boy, you've got a lovely voice."

"I am glad you think so, sir."

"You will prove a very valuable addition to my entertainments. I mean to show my appreciation, too. How much did I agree to give you?"

"Five dollars a week if business was good."

"It's bound to be good. I'll raise your wages to ten dollars a week, if you'll agree to sing one song, and two, if called for, at each of my evening entertainments."

"I'll do it, sir," said Harry, promptly. "It's a surprise to me, though, to find my voice so valuable to me."

"It's a popular gift, my boy; and all popular gifts are valuable. When I get my new bill printed, I must have your name on it."

They left Conway about noon the next day.

The Foxes, were destined to hear of Harry's success. The Conway Citizen was taken in the family, and, much to their astonishment, this is what they found, prominently placed, in the next number:

"The magical entertainment of Professor Hemenway, on Thursday evening, was even more successful than usual. He had had the good fortune to secure the services of a young vocalist named Harry Vane, who charmed both young and old by two popular selections. His voice and execution are both admirable, and we predict for him a brilliant future."

Mr. Fox read this aloud in evident wonder and excitement.

"Did you ever hear the like?" he said.

"Who'd have thought it?" chimed in Mrs. Fox.

CHAPTER VIII

A LIBERAL OFFER

Then commenced a round of travel—what the professor called a professional tour. By day they traveled in the wagon, carrying their paraphernalia with them, stopping at the principal towns, and giving evening entertainments. At many of these places the magician was well known, and his tricks were not new. But he had an attraction in his young assistant, who was regularly advertised on the posters as the "celebrated young vocalist, whose songs are everywhere received with admiring applause."

Indeed it was very near the truth. Harry was really a fine singer, and his fresh, attractive face and manly appearance won him a welcome in all the towns on their route. Sometimes a young girl in the audience threw him a bouquet. This made him blush and smile, and the donor felt rewarded.

Where was it going to end? Was he to continue in the service of the professor, and in time become himself a magician and a traveling celebrity? Harry was not sure about it. He saw that it would pay him better than most kinds of business, and he also discovered that Professor Hemenway was even better off than he had represented. Yet, he was not quite ready to select the same profession, but, being only sixteen, felt that he could afford to remain in it a while longer.

One day the professor gave him a surprise.

"Harry," he said, as they were jogging along a dusty road, "do you think you would like to travel?"

"I am traveling now," answered Harry, with a smile.

"True, but I don't mean that. Would you like to go on a long journey?"

"I should like nothing better," replied Harry, promptly.

"I'll tell you what I've been thinking about. I recently read in some paper that a man in my line had made a trip to Australia, and reaped a rich harvest. Everywhere he was received with enthusiasm, and made as much money, in one month as he would do here in four. Now why shouldn't I go to Australia?"

Harry's eyes sparkled.

"It would be a fine thing to do," he said.

"Then you would be willing to accompany me?"

"I would thank you for taking me," answered the boy.

"That is well!" said the professor, in a tone of satisfaction. "I confess I shouldn't like to go alone. It would be a great undertaking, but with a companion it would seem different. But, is there anyone who would object to your going?"

"Yes," answered Harry, smiling, "Mr. Fox, my 'guardeen,' would."

"We won't mind Mr. Fox. Very well, then, Harry, we will consider it settled. I shall rely on you to help me by your singing there as you do here. As to your wages, I may be able to pay you more."

"Never mind about that, professor. It will cost you a good deal to get us there. I am perfectly willing to work for the same sum I do now, or even less, on account of the extension of the trip."

"Then you leave that matter to me. I won't take advantage of your confidence, but you shall prosper if I do."

"How soon do you propose to go, professor?" asked Harry, with interest.

"As soon as possible. I shall ascertain when the first packet leaves Boston, and we will take passage in her."

The professor's decision pleased Harry. He had been a good scholar in geography—indeed, it was his favorite study—and had, besides, read as many books of travel as he could lay his hands on. Often he had wondered if it ever would be his fortune to see some of the distant countries of which he read with so much interest. Though he had cherished vague hopes, he had never really expected it. Now, however, the unattainable seemed within his grasp. He would not have to wait until he was a rich man, but when still a boy he could travel to the opposite side of the world, paying his expenses as he went along.

Two weeks passed. Each day they halted in some new place, and gave an evening performance. This life of constant motion had, at first, seemed strange to Harry. Now he was accustomed to it. He never felt nervous when he appeared before an audience to sing, but looked upon it as a matter of course.

At last they reached Boston. They were to give two entertainments at a hall at the south end. It was the first large city in which Harry had sung, but he received a welcome no less cordial than that which had been accorded to him in country towns.

They were staying at a modest hotel, comfortable, but not expensive. Harry was sitting in the reading room, when a servant brought in a card. It bore the rather remarkable name of

"DR. MENDELSSOHN BROWN."

"A gentleman to see you, Mr. Vane," said the servant.

Harry rose and surveyed the stranger in some surprise. He had long hair, of a reddish yellow, with an abundant beard of the same hue. His suit of worn black fitted him poorly, but Dr. Brown evidently was not a devotee of dress. No tailor could ever point to him, and say with pride: "That man's clothes were made at my shop."

"Do I speak to Mr. Harry Vane, the young vocalist?" asked the stranger, with a deferential smile.

"That's my name," answered our hero.

"You are alone?"

"Yes, sir," said Harry, a little puzzled.

"It is well. I will come to business at once. You have probably heard of me, eh?"

"Probably I have, but I do not remember names well."

"The name of Mendelssohn Brown, is pretty well known, I flatter myself," said the visitor, complacently. "To be brief—I heard you sing last evening, and was much pleased with your rendition of the various selections."

Harry bowed.

"I am about to form a juvenile Pinafore company, and would like to have you take the leading part. You would make an excellent Admiral. I propose to take my opera company all over the United States. I should be willing to pay you, as the star performer, twenty-five dollars a week."

Harry opened his eyes in amazement.

"Do you think me capable of singing in opera?" he asked.

"Yes, after being trained by your humble servant. What do you say?"

"I thank you for your flattering offer, Dr. Brown, but I don't feel at liberty to leave Professor Hemenway."

The doctor frowned.

"Let me tell you, you stand in your own light, Mr. Vane," he said, impatiently. "There is some difference between a common juggler, like the Magician of Madagascar,"—the doctor laughed ironically—"and a well-known musical director, who could make you famous. Does Hemenway pay you as much as I offer?"

"No, sir."

"I thought so. Then how can you hesitate?"

"We are about to make an Australian tour," answered Harry, "and, apart from all other considerations, I am glad to have a chance to travel."

"Couldn't you put it off?"

"No, sir."

"Then," said Dr. Brown, rather crestfallen, "I can only bid you good-morning. I think you are making a mistake."

"Perhaps, after I return from Australia, I might be ready to accept your offer."

"It will be too late," said the doctor, gloomily.

"Twenty-five dollars a week is large pay," thought Harry, "but I don't believe I should ever get it. Dr. Brown doesn't look much like a capitalist."

Half an hour later Professor Hemenway entered the hotel.

"Well, my boy," he said, "the die is cast! Next Saturday we sail from Long Wharf, bound for Australia."

"But professor, I have just had an offer of twenty-five dollars a week to sing in Pinafore."

"And have accepted!" exclaimed the magician in dismay.

"No; I respectfully declined. I would rather go with you."

"You shan't regret it, Harry!" said the professor, relieved. "If I am prosperous, you shall share in my prosperity."

"Thank you, professor; I am sure of that. What is the name of our vessel?"

"The Nantucket. It's a good, solid-looking craft, and I think it will bear us in safety to our destination."

CHAPTER IX

THE PASSENGERS

The Nantucket, Capt. Jabez Hill, master, was a large vessel, stanch and strong, and bore a good record, having been in service six years, and never having in that time met a serious disaster. It was a sailing vessel, and primarily intended to convey freight, but had accommodations for six passengers. Of these it had a full complement. Harry and the professor I name first, as those in whom we are most interested.

Next came John Appleton, a business man from Melbourne, who had visited the United States on business. He was a plain, substantial-looking person, of perhaps forty-five. Next came Montgomery Clinton, from Brooklyn, a young man of twenty-four, foolishly attired, who wore an eyeglass and anxiously aped the Londen swell, though born within sight of Boston State house. Harry regarded him with considerable amusement, and though he treated him with outward respect, mentally voted him very soft. Fifth on the list was a tall, sallow, thin individual, with a melancholy countenance, who was troubled with numerous symptoms, and was persuaded that he had not long to live. He was from Pennsylvania. He carried with him in his trunk a large assortment of pills and liquid medicines, one or another of which he took about once an hour. This gentleman's name was Marmaduke Timmins. Last came a tall, lean Yankee, the discoverer and proprietor of a valuable invention, which it was his purpose to introduce into Australia. Mr. Jonathan Stubbs, for this was his name, was by no means an undesirable addition to the little circle, and often excited a smile by his quaintly put and shrewd observations on topics of passing interest.

It was the third day at sea, when Harry, who had suffered but little from seasickness, came on deck, after a good dinner, and saw the dudish passenger, till now invisible, holding himself steady with an effort, and gazing sadly out upon the wild waste of waters without the help of his eyeglass.

"How do you feel, Mr. Clinton?" asked Harry.

"Horribly, Mr. Vane," answered Clinton, with a languid shudder. "I never thought it was such a bore, crossing the ocean, don't you know. I've a great idea of offering the captain a handsome sum to land somewhere, I don't care where."

"I don't think we shall go near any land, Mr. Clinton. I think you will have to make the best of it."

Hearing a step behind him, Harry turned, and his eyes rested on the melancholy countenance of Marmaduke Timmins, the chronic invalid.

"Good-morning, Mr. Timmins," said our hero. "I hope you stand the voyage well?"

"I've had several new symptoms since I came on board," responded Mr. Timmins, gloomily, "and I've made a dreadful discovery."

"What is it?" inquired Montgomery Clinton, in alarm.

"I find I've mislaid or forgotten to bring my box of Remedial pills. I don't know what I shall do without them."

"I've got a box of Brandeth's pills downstairs," said Clinton. "You're welcome to a part of them, I'm sure."

"They wouldn't do! What can you be thinking of, young man? Do you think there's no difference between pills?"

"I'm sure I can't tell, don't you know?"

"Young man, you are sadly ignorant," said Timmins, severely. "I've got five other kinds of pills downstairs, for different maladies I am subject to, but none of them will take the place of Remedial pills."

"Will any of them cure seasickness?" asked the dude, eagerly.

"I can give you a remedy for seasickness, Mr. Clinton," said Mr. Holdfast, the mate, who chanced to overhear the inquiry.

"What is it, Mr. Holdfast? I shall be really grateful, I assure you, if you can cure that beastly malady."

"Swallow a piece of raw salt pork about an inch square," said the mate gravely, "and follow it up by a glass of sea water, taken at a gulp."

"That's horrid, awfully horrid!" gasped Clinton, shuddering, and looking very pale. "It actually makes me sick to think of it, don't you know," and he retreated to the cabin, with one hand pressed on his stomach.

"That young man's a fool!" said Mr. Timmins. "He knows no more about pills than a baby."

"Nor do I, Mr. Timmins," said Harry, smiling.

"I pity you then. My life has been saved several times by pills."

"I'd rather live without them."

Marmaduke sadly shook his head as he walked away.

"That man's a walking drug store," said the mate, looking after him. "I'd rather go to Davy's locker, and be done with it, than to fill myself up with pills and potions."

"You're looking chipper, my boy," said a newcomer, in a nasal voice. "Haven't been seasick, I guess."

Harry recognized the voice of the Yankee inventor, Jonathan Stubbs.

"No, sir; I have had very little trouble."

"I'm goin' to get up a cure for seasickness when I have time—a kind of a self-acting, automatic belt—I guess there'd be plenty of money in it."

"It would be a great blessing, Mr. Stubbs. Poor Mr. Clinton would no doubt be glad to buy it."

"Do you mean that languishin' creeter with an eyeglass and spindle legs? What are such fellows made for?"

"Rather for ornament than use," answered Harry, gravely.

The Yankee burst into a loud guffaw, and regarded Harry's remark a capital joke.

The voyage was to be a long one, and after a couple of weeks they all had their sea legs on. All had become acquainted, and settled down to a regular routine. But the time dragged, and as there were no morning or evening papers, something seemed necessary to break the monotony.

"Harry," said the professor, "I have an idea."

"What is it, professor?"

"Suppose we give an exhibition for the benefit of our fellow passengers and the crew."

"I am ready to do my part."

"Then I will speak to the captain."

The result was that on the first quiet day Professor Hemenway and his assistant gave a matinee performance on the deck of the Nantucket, at which all who could possibly be spared were present. To some of the sailors it was a novelty, and the magician's tricks actually inspired some with the feeling that he was possessed of supernatural powers.

"Will you lend me your hat, Mr. Clinton?" he asked presently, of the dude.

"Certainly, professor," drawled the young man.

The professor took it, and tapped it.

"Are you sure there is nothing in it?" he asked.

"I am sure of it. Really, I don't carry things in my hat, don't you know."

"What do you say to this, then?" and Professor Hemenway drew out of the hat half a dozen onions, a couple of potatoes, and a ship biscuit.

"My dear sir, I think you are mistaken," he said. "I see you carry your lunch in your hat."

All present laughed at the horrified face of the dude.

"On my honor, I don't know how those horrid things came in my hat," he stammered.

"Are you fond of onions, Mr. Clinton?" asked Harry.

"I wouldn't eat one for—for a new suit of clothes!" protested Clinton, earnestly.

"Allow me to return your hat, Mr. Clinton," said the professor, politely. "I suppose you want the vegetables too. Here are the onions, and the rest."

"They are not mine, on my honor," said Clinton, very much embarrassed. "Here, my good man, can you make use of these?"

The sailor whom he addressed accepted the gift with a grin.

"Thank you kindly, sir," he said, "If so be as I ain't a-robbin' you."

"I have no use for them, my good man. I never ate an onion in my life."

"Then I don't think you know what's good," said Mr. Stubbs. "An onion, let me tell you, is mighty good eatin', and healthy, too."

At the close of the magical entertainment, Harry sang by request, and no part of the performance was more popular. He received many warm congratulations.

"Really, Mr. Vane, you sing like a nightingale, don't you know," was the tribute of Clinton.

"Bless me!" said Mr. Timmins; "I was so absorbed in your song that I have forgotten to take my catarrh medicine."

"Thank you, sir; that is the best compliment I have received," returned Harry, with a smile.

Little has been said thus far of Captain Hill, the chief officer of the Nantucket. He was a stout, red-faced seaman, nearing fifty years of age, and had been in service ever since he was fifteen. He was a thorough sailor, and fitted in every way but one to take charge of a ship bound to any part of the world. His one disqualification may be stated briefly—he had a passion for drink.

It was not immediately that this was found out. He took his meals with the passengers, but it was not then that he indulged his appetite. He kept a private store of liquors in his cabin, and had recourse to them when by himself, under the impression that he could keep it a secret. But intemperance, like murder, will out.

Harry and the professor were standing by the rail looking out at sea, one day, when a thick voice greeted them, "Good-mor'n', gentlemen," this address being followed by a hiccough. Both turned quickly, and exchanged a significant glance when they recognized the captain.

"Yes," answered Professor Hemenway, "it is indeed a fine morning."

"I am sorry to see this, Harry," said the professor.

"Yes, sir; it is a pity any gentleman should drink too much."

"Yes, but that isn't all," said the professor, earnestly; "it is a pity, of course, that Captain Hill should so sin against his own health, but we must consider furthermore, that he has our lives under his control. Our safety depends on his prudent management."

"He seems to understand his business," said Harry.

"Granted; but no man, however good a seaman, is fit to manage a vessel when he allows liquor to rob him of his senses. I wish I had had a knowledge beforehand of the captain's infirmity."

"Suppose you had, sir?"

"I wouldn't have trusted myself on board the Nantucket, you may be sure of that."

"It may be only an exceptional case."

"Let us hope so."

The next occasion on which the captain displayed his infirmity was rather a laughable one. He came up from the cabin about three o'clock in the afternoon so full that he was forced to stagger as he walked. Directly in front of him the young dude, Montgomery Clinton, was pacing the deck, carrying in his hand a rattan cane such as he used on shore. As he overhauled him, Captain Hill, with the instinct of a drunken man, locked arms with the young man, and forced him to promenade in his company, talking rather incoherently meanwhile. Clinton's look of distress and perplexity, as he submitted to his fate, caused Harry nearly to explode with laughter. They were indeed a singular pair.

Finally there came a disaster. A lurch of the vessel proved too much for the captain, who, in losing his equilibrium, also upset Clinton, and the two rolled down under one of the ship's boats, which was slung on one side.

Montgomery Clinton picked himself up, and hurriedly betook himself to his cabin, fearing that he might fall again into the clutches of his unwelcome companion. The captain was helped to his feet by the mate, and was persuaded also to go downstairs.

"The captain was pretty well slewed, professor," said Mr. Stubbs, who chanced to be on deck at the time.

"It looks like it," answered Professor Hemenway.

"If he does that often it'll be a bad lookout for us."

"Just what I am thinking, Mr. Stubbs."

CHAPTER X

THE YOUNG SAILOR

The crew of the Nantucket consisted of twelve sailors and a boy, not counting the officers. This boy was about Harry's age, but an inch or two shorter, and with great breadth of shoulders. He had a good-natured face, and was a general favorite on board, as is apt to be the case with a boy, if he possesses any attractive qualities. He came from New Hampshire and he was known as Jack.

It was natural that Harry, as the only other boy on board, though a passenger, should be attracted to Jack. He took an opportunity when Jack was off duty to have a chat with him.

"How long have you been a sailor, Jack?" he asked.

"Three years; I first went to sea when I was thirteen."

"How did you happen to go in the first place?"

"I may say to begin with, that I always liked the water. I was born in a little village bordering Lake Winnipiseogee, and was out on the lake whenever I could get the chance, either in a rowboat or sailboat. I felt as much at home on the water as on the land. Still, I never should have gone to sea had it not been for my stepfather."

"Then you have a stepfather?"

"Yes. My father died when I was ten, leaving my mother a little farm and a comfortable house. I was a young boy, and it is hard for a woman to carry on a farm. A man came into town, and started in some small business. He pretended that he had money, but I guess he had precious little. At any rate, he didn't object to more. Pretty soon he fixed his eyes on our farm, and, finding that mother owned it clear, he got to coming round pretty often. I never liked him, though he pretended to be fond of me, and used to pat me on the head, and bring me candy. I wondered what made him come so often, but I didn't mistrust anything till one day mother called me and said she had something important to say to me.

"'Jack,' she said, 'what do you think of Mr. Bannock?'

"'I don't think much of him,' I answered.

"'He is to be your father, Jack. I have promised to marry him.'

"'You may marry him,' I answered hotly, 'but he will be no father of mine. My father lies in the churchyard. I wish he were alive again.'

"'So do I, Jack' said mother, wiping her eyes, 'but we know that can't be.'"

"How did he treat you, Jack?" asked Harry, interested.

"He never liked me, and I didn't like him at all He tried to impose upon me, and order me round, but he didn't make out much. Still, he was always annoying me in mean little ways, and finally I got all I could stand, and the long and short of it is that I ran away to Portsmouth, and went on a coasting voyage. After I got back I shipped from Boston for Liverpool, and ever since I've kept sailing in one direction or another. This will be my longest voyage."

"Haven't you been to see your mother since you left home three years ago?" Harry inquired.

"Of course I have," said Jack, promptly. "I always go to see her as soon as I get home from a voyage. Poor mother! She was looking pale and thin when I saw her three weeks ago. I am sure she has repented marrying, but she won't own up. When I'm a man——"

"Well, Jack; when you're a man?"

"I'll see that she has a better time, and if old Bannock don't like it he can clear out. I think he will anyway."

"Clear out?"

"Yes; he will have spent all the property by that time, and when that is done, he won't make much objection to going away. Then I will take care of mother, and see that she does not suffer for anything."

"You are right, Jack. I sympathize with you. I hope you'll succeed. I only wish I had a mother to look out for," and Harry's fine face wore an expression of sadness. "But there's one thing I can't help saying, though I don't want to discourage you."

"What is that, Harry?"

"I don't see how you are going to lay up much money in going before the mast. Your pay must be small."

"It is. I only earn ten dollars a month," replied Jack.

"And out of that you must buy your clothes?"

"Yes, that's true."

"Then how do you expect to better yourself?" asked Harry, looking perplexed.

"I'll tell you, if you won't say anything about it," answered Jack, in a lower tone.

"Go ahead."

"We are going to Australia, you know. I've heard there are good chances of making money there, in mining or herding cattle, and I mean to leave the ship at Melbourne. Of course, I don't want anything said about it."

"Do you think the captain would try to prevent you, Jack?"

"I think he would. He don't like me, at any rate."

"Why not?"

"That is more than I can tell, but I can see that he has a prejudice against me."

The boys were so absorbed in their talk that they did not notice the approach of the captain till his harsh voice was heard.

"What are you two boys chattering about?" he demanded, with a frown.

Jack turned round startled, but Harry faced the captain calmly, and did not speak.

"Will you answer me?" he repeated, raising his voice.

"I was talking about home and my mother," said Jack.

"Mighty interesting, upon my word! And what were you talking about?" continued Captain Hill, turning to Harry.

"That can be of no interest to you, Captain Hill," said Harry, coldly. "You appear to forget that I am a passenger."

As he walked away, the captain regarded him with an ominous scowl. He wished that for fifteen minutes Harry had been one of the crew. It was fortunate for Jack that his temper was diverted, for, apparently forgetting the young sailor, he strode on, and Jack managed to slip down to the forecastle.

This was not by any means the last conversation Harry had with Jack Pendleton—for this he found to be the young sailor's name—and they soon became excellent friends.

"Jack," said Harry, one day, "I never should take you to be a sailor if I met you on land."

"Why not?"

"Because you talk like a well-educated boy."

"So I am. I was always fond of my books, and stood high in school. But for my stepfather I might be there yet. As it is, my education stopped at the age of thirteen."

"Not necessarily. You have learned a good deal since."

"Yes, but not of books. I hope sometime to be able to continue my studies. At present it is my business to learn seamanship."

Harry had the more time on his hands, as his traveling companion, the professor, took sick, and was confined for three or four weeks to his cabin. There was no danger, but still the ship's surgeon advised him to stay below.

"What makes you keep company with that boy, Mr. Vane?" asked Montgomery Clinton, who would have liked more of Harry's society himself.

"Why shouldn't I?"

"Because he is a common sailor, don't you know."

"I think he is rather an uncommon sailor. He is very well educated."

"Oh, yes; I suppose he can read and write; but, of course, he can never be admitted into society, don't you know?"

"No, I don't, Mr. Clinton. He may be a captain some day."

"But he isn't now. I give you my word, I noticed this morning, when you were speaking with him, that his fingers were all soiled with tar. That's horrid, don't you know."

"Don't you think he's a good-looking boy, Mr. Clinton?"

"Well, yes; I suppose, for one of the lower order, Mr. Vane."

"You forget we don't have any distinction of classes in America."

"Don't we though? By Jove! Mr. Vane, you don't put yourself on a level with those creatures that dig ditches and climb masts, and such things?"

"Your sentiments are very undemocratic, Mr. Clinton. You ought to have been born in England."

"I wish I had been. I like their institutions a good deal better than ours, don't you know?"

"When I first spoke with you, Mr. Clinton, I thought you might be an Englishman."

"Did you, really?" inquired Clinton, with evident pleasure. "I'm often taken for an Englishman, on my honor. I don't know why it is, but positively, I'm often asked when I came from the other side."

"Would you rather be taken for an Englishman than an American?"

"Well, you see, there are some Americans that are so vulgar, don't you know—talk through their noses, and all that."

"Where were you born, Mr. Clinton?"

"In Massachusetts, not far from Boston."

"By the way, Mr. Vane, are you descended from Sir Henry Vane, one of the royal governors of Massachusetts? I have been meaning to ask you."

"I can't tell you, Mr. Clinton; but my name happens to be the same—Harry."

"Really, that is very interesting. I should think you would look up the matter."

"Perhaps I will when I return home!" said Harry, who cared very little about the matter. From this time, however, Clinton regarded him with increased respect, and manifested an increased liking for his society, from his supposed aristocratic lineage. Our hero treated him with good-natured toleration, but much preferred the company of Jack Pendleton, sailor as he was, though his fingers were not infrequently smeared with tar. Harry did not mind this; but was attracted by the frank, good-humored face of young Jack, and was always glad to have a chat with him. He had a chance, though at considerable personal risk, to do him a signal service before long.

The captain's habits, it must be said, did not improve. His stock of liquor was ample, and he continued to indulge himself. Generally he kept within safe bounds, but at times he allowed his appetite to get the better of him. Whenever that happened, it was fortunate if he drank himself into a state of stupefaction, and remained in his cabin, leaving the management of the ship to the mate, Mr. Holdfast, who was thoroughly temperate. Unfortunately, he was not always content to remain in the cabin. He would stagger upstairs and give orders which might or might not, be judicious.

One day—it was about a month after they left port—Captain Hill came up on deck in one of his worst fits of intoxication. All the passengers were on deck, it being a fair day. They regarded the captain with alarm, for in his hand he held a pistol, which he carried in such careless style that it might be discharged at any time.

Jack Pendleton had been sent up to the masthead on some duty by the mate. The captain's roving eyes fell upon him, and the dislike he felt for the boy found vent.

"What are you doing up there, you young lubber?" he shouted.

"Mr. Holdfast sent me," answered Jack.

"You lie!" roared the captain. "I'll teach you to lie to me!"

"I'll come down, sir," said Jack, "if you say so."

"I'll bring you down!" shouted the captain, furiously, as he deliberately pointed the pistol at the cabin boy, and prepared to pull the trigger.

There was a cry of horror on the part of the passengers as they saw the insane act of the captain, and realized the peril of poor Jack. But, in spite of all, the boy would probably have fallen a victim to the drunken fury of Captain Hill. Jack himself fully understood his danger, and his ruddy face turned pale. His life hung in the balance, and was saved only by the courage of his boy friend, Harry.

Of all the passengers, Harry stood nearest to the captain. When he saw the pistol pointed at Jack, he did not stop to think, but made a bound, and dashed the weapon from the captain's hand. It was discharged but the bullet sped over the rail and dropped into the ocean. Nor did Harry stop here. He seized the fallen pistol, and hurled it over the side of the vessel.

The captain was for the moment stupefied by the suddenness of the act. Then, in a voice of fury, he exclaimed, pointing to Harry: "Put that boy in irons!"

CHAPTER XI

A SENSATIONAL SCENE

"Put that boy in irons!" repeated Captain Hill, his eyes blazing with anger.

Not a sailor stirred. There was not one that did not admire Harry's promptness, which had saved Jack's life, and prevented the captain from becoming a murderer.

"Here, you two men, seize the boy, and carry him below!" exclaimed the captain, addressing Brown and Higgins, the two sailors nearest.

The two men looked at each other, moved a step forward, and then stopped.

"Is this mutiny?" roared the captain, with a bloodcurdling oath. "Am I master in my own ship or not?"

What might have been the issue is hard to tell, had not the Yankee passenger already referred to, Jonathan Stubbs, come forward and taken up the gauntlet.

"Look here, cap'n," he commenced, in a drawling tone, "what's all this fuss you're kickin' up? You're kinder riled, ain't you?"

"Who are you that dare to bandy words with me? Men, do you hear me? Put that boy in irons, or must I do it myself?"

"Look here, cap'n, let's argy that matter a little," said Stubbs. "What's the boy to be put in irons for?"

"For grossly insulting me, and defying my authority."

"He has prevented your committing murder, if that's what you mean. You ought to thank him."

"Take care, sir!" thundered the captain, "or I may put you in irons, also."

"I reckon you might find a little opposition," said the Yankee, quietly. "I'm a passenger on this vessel, Captain Hill, and your authority doesn't extend to me."

"We'll see about that, sir," said the captain, and he grasped Stubbs by the collar.

Now, the Yankee was not a heavy man, but he was very strong and wiry, and, moreover, in his early days, like Abraham Lincoln, he had been the best wrestler in the Vermont village in which he was born. He was a very quiet, peaceable man, but he was accustomed to resent insult in an effective way. He wrenched himself free by a powerful effort; then, with a dexterous movement of one of his long legs, he tripped up the captain, who fell in a heap upon the deck. The shock, added to the effects of his intoxication, seemed to stupefy the captain, who remained where he fell.

"Boys," said Stubbs, coolly, to the two sailors, who had been ordered to put Harry in irons, "hadn't you better help the captain into his cabin? He seems to be unwell."

Just then the mate came on deck. He didn't make inquiries, but took in the situation at a glance, and assisted the captain to his feet.

"Shall I help you downstairs, sir?" he asked.

The captain silently acquiesced, and the prime actor in this rather startling scene left the deck.

Jack Pendleton scrambled down from his elevated perch with the agility of a cat. He ran up to Harry, and grasped his hand with evident emotion.

"You have saved my life!" he said. "I will always be your friend. I would lay down my life for you."

"It's all right, Jack," said Harry, rather shyly. "You would have done the same for me."

"Yes, I would," answered Jack, heartily, "But there's no one else who would have done it for me."

"Are you going to leave me out, my boy?" asked the Yankee, with a smile on his plain but good-natured face.

"No, sir," responded Jack. "You stood up to the captain like a man. He didn't frighten you."

"No, I wasn't much scared," drawled Stubbs, contorting his features drolly. "But, I say, young man, I've got a piece of advice to give you. You don't seem to be much of a favorite with the captain."

"It doesn't look so," said Jack, laughing in spite of the danger through which he had passed.

"Just you keep out of his way as much as you can. When a man gets as full as he does, he's apt to be dangerous."

"Thank you, sir; I will."

Among the spectators of the scene just described, the most panic-stricken, probably was Montgomery Clinton, the Brooklyn dude.

After the captain had gone below, he walked up to Harry, whom he regarded with evident admiration.

"I say, you're quite a hero. I was awfully frightened, don't you know, when that big bully aimed at the sailor boy."

"You looked a little nervous, Mr. Clinton," said Harry, smiling.

"You were awfully brave, to knock the pistol out of his hand. I don't see how you dared to do it."

"I didn't stop to think of danger. I saw that Jack's life was in danger, and I did the only thing I could to save him."

"I'm glad you're not put in irons. It must be awful to be in irons."

"I don't think I should like it, though I never had any experience. You'd have stood by me, wouldn't you, Mr. Clinton?"

Clinton was evidently alarmed at the suggestion.

"Yes, of course," he said, nervously; "that is, I would have gone down to see you on the sly. You wouldn't expect me to fight the captain, don't you know."

Harry could hardly refrain from smiling at the idea of the spindle-shaped dude resisting the captain; but he kept a straight face as he answered:

"I look upon you as a brave man, Mr. Clinton. When I get into trouble, I shall be sure to call upon you."

"Oh, certainly," stammered Clinton. "But I say, Mr. Vane, I hope you'll be prudent; I do, really. Captain Hill might shoot you, you know, as he tried to shoot the sailor boy just now."

"If he does, Mr. Clinton, I shall expect you to interfere, You are not as strong as the captain, but a bold front will go a great way. If you threaten to—to horsewhip him, I think it might produce an effect upon him."

"Really, my dear Mr. Vane," said Clinton, turning pale, "I don't think I could go as far as that."

"I thought you were my friend, Mr. Clinton," said Harry, reproachfully.

"So I am, but I think you are, too—too bloodthirsty, Mr. Vane. It is best to be prudent, don't you know. There's that Yankee, Mr. Stubbs; he would do a great deal better than I. He's stronger, and older, and—you'd better speak to him, don't you know."

"A very good suggestion, Mr. Clinton," said Harry.

"I am afraid I should fare badly," thought our hero, "if I depended upon Clinton to stand by me. He isn't of the stuff they make heroes of."

Twenty-four hours passed before Captain Hill reappeared on deck. Meanwhile Harry had received congratulations from all the passengers on his display of pluck, and from some of the sailors besides. In fact, if he had not been a sensible boy, he might have been in danger of being spoiled by praise. But he answered, very modestly, that he had only acted from impulse, actuated by a desire to save Jack, and had not had time to count the consequences.

"I'll stand by you, my lad," said Hirman Stubbs. "The captain may try to do you wrong, but he will have somebody else to reckon with—I won't see you hurt."

"Thank you, Mr. Stubbs," said Harry, heartily. "I know the value of your help already. Mr. Clinton also is willing to stand by me, though he says he don't want to get into a fight with the captain."

"Clinton! That spindle-legged dude!" said Stubbs, exploding with laughter. "My! he couldn't scare a fly."

Harry laughed, too. He could not help doing so.

"He seems a good fellow, though not exactly a hero," he said. "I am glad to have his good will."

"He is more of a tailor's dummy than a man," said Stubbs. "I always want to laugh when I look at him. Hist! there's the captain."

Harry turned quickly toward the companionway, and saw Captain Hill set foot on the deck. A glance satisfied him that the captain was sober.

CHAPTER XII

A STORM

Captain Hill must have observed Harry and Mr. Stubbs, but walked by them without notice, and attended to his duties, giving his orders in a sharp quick tone. He was an experienced seaman, and thoroughly fitted for the post of chief, when not under the influence of liquor.
"I am glad to see that the captain is sober," said Stubbs, in a low voice.
"So am I," answered Harry.
One change, all noticed in Captain Hill. He became silent, reserved, morose. His orders were given in a quick, peremptory tone, and he seemed to cherish a grudge against all on board. Some captains add much to the pleasure of the passengers by their social and cheery manners, but whenever Captain Hill appeared, a wet blanket seemed to fall on the spirits of passengers and crew, and they conversed in an undertone, as if under restraint.
Between the captain and the mate there was a great difference. Mr. Holdfast had a bluff, hearty way with him, which made him popular with all on board. As an officer, he was strict, and expected his orders to be executed promptly, but in private he was affable and agreeable. The sailors felt instinctively that he was their friend, and regarded him with attachment, while they respected his seamanship. If a vote had been taken, there was not one but would have preferred him as captain to Captain Hill.
Thus far—I am speaking of a time when the Nantucket was three months out—there had been no serious storm. Rough weather there had been, and wet, disagreeable weather, but the staunch ship had easily overcome all the perils of the sea, and, with the exception of Montgomery Clinton, no one had been seriously alarmed. But one afternoon a cloud appeared in the hitherto clear sky, which would have attracted no attention from a landsman. Mr. Holdfast observed it, however, and, quietly calling the captain, directed his attention to it.
"I think we are going to have a bad storm, Captain Hill," he said. "That's a weather breeder."
The captain watched the cloud for a moment, and then answered, quietly: "I think you are right, Mr. Holdfast. You may give your orders accordingly."
The sails were reefed, and the vessel was prepared for the warfare with the elements which awaited it.
The little cloud increased portentiously in size. All at once a strong wind sprang up, the sea roughened, and the billows grew white with fury, while the good ship, stanch as she was, creaked and groaned and was tossed as if it were a toy boat on the wrathful ocean.
The passengers were all seriously alarmed. They had never before realized what a storm at sea was. Even a man of courage may well be daunted by the terrific power of the sea when it is roused to such an exhibition.
"Harry," said the professor, "this is terrible."
"Yes, indeed," answered the boy, gravely.
It became so rough and difficult to stand on deck, on account of the vessel being tossed about like a cockleshell, that Harry felt constrained to go below.
As he passed the cabin of Montgomery Clinton, he heard a faint voice call his name.
Entering, he saw the dude stretched out in his berth, with an expression of helpless terror in his weak face.

"Oh! Mr. Vane," he said; "do you think we are going to the bottom?"

"I hope not, Mr. Clinton. Our officers are skillful men. They will do all they can for us."

It was a terrible night. None of the passengers ventured upon deck. Indeed, such was the motion that it would have been dangerous, as even the sailors found it difficult to keep their footing. Harry was pale and quiet, unlike his friend from Brooklyn, whose moans were heard mingled with the noise of the tempest.

It was about three o'clock in the morning when those below heard, with terror, a fearful crash, and a trampling of feet above. One of the masts had fallen before the fury of the storm, and the shock made the good ship careen to a dangerous extent. What happened, however, was not understood below.

"I wonder what has happened," said the professor, nervously. "I think I will go up and see."

He got out of his berth, but only to be pitched helpless to the other end of the cabin.

"This is terrible!" he said, as he picked himself up.

"I will try my luck, professor," said Harry.

He scrambled out of his berth, and, with great difficulty, made his way upstairs.

One glance told him what had occurred. The crippled ship was laboring through the sea. It seemed like a very unequal combat, and Harry might be excused for deciding that the ship was doomed. All about the sea wore its fiercest aspect. Harry returned cautiously to his cabin.

"Well?" said the professor.

"One of the masts is gone," answered the boy. "The ship is having a hard time."

"Is there danger?" asked the professor, anxiously.

"I am afraid so," said Harry, gravely.

At length the night wore away. The violence of the storm seemed to have abated, for, after a time, the motion diminished. More enterprising than the rest of the passengers, Harry resolved to go on deck.

"Won't you come with me, Mr. Clinton?" he asked.

"I—I couldn't, 'pon my honor. I'm as weak as a rag. I don't think I could get out of my berth, really, now."

"I'll go with you, my young friend," said Mr. Stubbs.

Harry and his Yankee friend set foot cautiously on deck. The prospect was not reassuring. The ship rolled heavily, and from the creaking it seemed that the timbers of the hull were strained. The sailors looked fagged out, and there was a set, stern look on the face of the captain, whom, nevertheless, Mr. Stubbs ventured to accost.

"What's the prospect, captain?" he asked.

"You'd better make your will," said the captain, grimly.

"That's cheerful," commented Stubbs, turning to Harry.

"Yes, sir," answered Harry, soberly.

"Don't tell our foppish friend below, or he'll rend our ears with his howls. But you, my young friend, it's rather rough on you. How old are you?"

"Sixteen."

"And I'm rising fifty. Even if I am taken away, I've had a good thirty years the advantage of you. I've had a good time, on the whole, and enjoyed myself as well as the average. Still, I don't quite like going to the bottom in the Nantucket. I was looking forward to at least twenty years or so more of life."

"We must submit to the will of God," said Harry.

"You are quite right, my boy! It is easy to see that you have been well trained. Mr. Holdfast"—for they had reached the place where the mate was standing—"shall we outlive the storm?"

"It is hard to say, Mr. Stubbs. It depends on the stanchness of the ship. We'll do all we can."

Ten minutes later there was a sinister answer to the inquiry of Mr. Stubbs. A sailor, who had been sent down into the hold, came with the information that the ship had sprung a leak.

Then commenced the weary work at the pumps. The sailors were already worn out with fighting the storm under the direction of the captain and mate, and it seemed almost more than flesh and blood could stand to undertake the additional labor.

Harry and Mr. Stubbs had a hurried conference.

"Can't we help at this work, Mr. Stubbs?" asked Harry. "The poor men look utterly exhausted."

"Well thought of, my boy! I am with you. I will speak to the captain."

But Mr. Holdfast, the mate, chanced to be nearer, and to him Mr. Stubbs put the question: "Can't I help at the pumps?"

"And I, too, Mr. Holdfast," put in Harry.

"I accept your offer with thanks. The men are very tired."

So Harry and Mr. Stubbs helped at this necessary work, and when the professor and the Melbourne merchant heard of it they, too, volunteered. But Marmaduke Timmins, the valetudinarian, and Montgomery Clinton felt quite inadequate to the task.

Harry found his work tiresome and fatiguing, but he had the comfort of feeling that he was relieving the exhausted sailors, and doing something to save his own life and the lives of his companions.

He caught sight of poor Jack, looking ready to drop.

"Jack, you must be very tired," he said, in a tone of deep sympathy.

"If I stood still I should drop on the deck fast asleep," said Jack.

"Can't you lie down for an hour? I am taking your place."

Mr. Holdfast coming up at this moment, Harry suggested this to him, and the mate said kindly:

"Jack, my lad, go below and catch a little nap. I will call you when I want you."

So Jack, much relieved, went below, and, without a thought of the danger, so fatigued was he, fell asleep the moment he got into his bunk, and was not called up for four hours.

After a while they reduced the flow of water, but ascertained that the ship was badly strained, and by no means safe. It was not till the next day, however, that an important decision was reached.

All were called on deck.

"It is my duty to tell you," said Captain Hill, "that the ship is so damaged by the recent storm that it is liable to sink at any time. Those who choose to run the risk may remain, however. I propose, with such as choose to join me, to take to the boats. I will give you fifteen minutes to decide."

Excitement and dismay were painted on the faces of all. The ship might be insecure, but to launch out upon the great ocean in a frail boat seemed to involve still greater danger.

CHAPTER XIII

"WHO WILL STAY?"

The decision was a momentous one. It might be death to remain on the ship, but to a landsman it seemed still more perilous to embark on an angry sea in a frail boat.

The passengers looked at each other in doubt and perplexity.

They had but fifteen minutes in which to make up their minds.

The mate stood by, his face and manner serious and thoughtful.

"Mr. Holdfast," said Mr. Stubbs, "do you agree with the captain that it is our best course to take to the boats?"

"I should prefer to try the ship a little longer. I say so with diffidence, since the captain has a longer experience than I."

"I don't think much of your judgment, Mr. Holdfast," said Captain Hill, in a tone of contempt.

The mate's face flushed—not so much at the words as the tone.

"Nevertheless Captain Hill," he said, "I stand by what I have said."

"Mr. Holdfast," said Mr. Stubbs, who seemed to speak for the passengers, "if some of us decide to remain on the ship, will you remain with us?"

"I will!" answered the mate, promptly.

"Then set me down as the first to remain," said Stubbs.

Somehow this man, rough and abrupt as he was, had impressed Harry as a man in whom confidence might be reposed. He felt safe in following where he led.

"I am but a boy," he said, "but I have to decide for my life. I shall remain with the mate and Mr. Stubbs."

Quietly Stubbs shook hands with Harry.

"I am glad to have you with us," he said earnestly. "We will die or live together."

Next came Professor Hemenway.

"Put me down as the third," he said. "Harry, we sailed together, and we will remain together to the end."

"I go in the boat," said John Appleton. "I have a great respect for Mr. Holdfast, but I defer to the captain's judgment as superior."

He went over and ranged himself beside the captain.

"You are a sensible man, sir," said Captain Hill, with a scornful glance at the mate and the passengers who sided with him. "Mr. Holdfast can go down with the ship, if he desires. I prefer to cut loose from a doomed vessel."

Marmaduke Timmins, the invalid, looked more sallow and nervous than ever. He had swallowed a pill while the others were speaking, to give himself confidence.

"I will go with the captain," he said. "My life is likely to be short, for my diseases are many, but I owe it to myself to do my best to save it."

"In deciding to go with me, you are doing your best, sir," said Captain Hill.

He had not hitherto paid much attention to Mr. Timmins, whom he looked upon as a crank on the subject of health, but he was disposed to look upon him now with more favor.

At this moment Montgomery Clinton appeared at the head of the stairs. The poor fellow was pale, and disheveled, and tottered from weakness.

"What's going on?" he asked, feebly. Harry took it upon himself to explain, using as few words as possible.

"Will you go with the captain, or stay on the Nantucket?" asked Harry.

"Really, I couldn't stand sailing in a little boat, you know."

"That's settled, then!" said the captain. "Into the boats with you!"

The sailors and two passengers lowered themselves into the long boat, which was large enough to receive them all, till only Jack Pendleton and the captain remained.

"Get in, boy!" said the captain, harshly.

Jack stepped back, and said, manfully: "I will remain on board the ship, sir."

While this discussion had been going on, the boat was being stored with kegs of water and provisions, and soon after the sailors began to ply the oars.

The little band that remained looked silently and solemnly, as they saw their late companions borne farther and farther away from them on the crested waves.

"It's a question which will last longer, the ship or the boat," said Mr. Holdfast.

"We must work—I know that," said Mr. Stubbs. "Captain Holdfast, I salute you as my commander. Give us your orders."

"Are you all agreed, gentlemen?" asked Holdfast.

"We are," answered all except Montgomery Clinton, who was clinging to the side with a greenish pallor on his face.

"Then I shall set you to work at the pumps. Jack I assign you and the professor to duty first. You will work an hour; then Mr. Stubbs and Mr. Vane will relieve you. I will look out for the vessel's course."

"I am afraid I couldn't pump," said Montgomery Clinton. "I feel so awfully weak, you know, I think I'm going to die!"

Harry looked out to sea and saw the little boat containing the remnant of their company growing smaller and smaller. A sudden feeling of loneliness overcame him, and he asked himself, seriously: "Is death, then, so near?"

The sea was still rough, but the violence of the storm was past. In a few hours the surface of the sea was much less agitated. The spirits of the passengers rose, especially after learning from the mate that he had been able to stop the leak, through the experience which he acquired in his younger days as assistant to a ship carpenter.

"Then the old ship is likely to float a while longer?" said Mr. Stubbs, cheerfully.

"Not a short time, either, if the weather continues favorable."

"Captain Hill was in too much of a hurry to leave the vessel," remarked Harry.

"Yes," answered Holdfast. "Such was my opinion when I thought the Nantucket in much worse condition than at present. If the captain and sailors had remained on board, we could have continued our voyage to Melbourne without difficulty."

"And now?" said Mr. Stubbs, interrogatively.

"Now we have no force to man her. Little Jack and myself are the only sailors on board."

"But not the only men."

"That is true. I think, however, that you or the professor would find it rather hard to spread or take in sail."

Mr. Stubbs looked up into the rigging and shrugged his shoulders.

The next day Mr. Clinton appeared on deck. He looked faded and played out, but he was no longer the woebegone creature of a day or two previous. Even he turned out to be of use, for he knew something about cooking, and volunteered to assist in preparing the meals, the ship's cook having left the ship with the captain. Accordingly, he rose in the estimation of the passengers—having proved that he was not wholly a drone.

Jack and Harry grew still more intimate. The young sailor was under no restraint now that the captain was not on board, for with the mate he had always been a favorite.

All efforts were made to keep the ship on her course. They could not put up all the sails, however, and made but slow progress. They did little but drift. Nor did they encounter any other vessel for several days, so that there was no chance of obtaining the desired assistance.

"I wonder where it will all end, Jack?" said Harry, one evening.

"I don't trouble myself much about that, Harry," said the young sailor. "I am content as I am."

"Don't you look ahead, then?"

"I am happy with you and the few we have on board. They are kind to me; what more do I need?"

"I can't be contented so easily, Jack. I hope there is a long life before us. Here we are, making no progress. We are doing nothing to advance ourselves."

But this did not make much impression on Jack. He did not look beyond the present, and so that this was comfortable, he left the future to look out for itself.

"What do you think has become of Captain Hill and his companions, Mr. Holdfast?" asked Mr. Stubbs, on the third evening after the separation.

"He is probably still afloat, unless he has been fortunate enough to be picked up by some vessel."

"There is no hope of reaching land in the Nantucket is there," continued Mr. Stubbs.
"There is considerable fear of it," said the mate.
"Why do you use the word fear?" asked Stubbs, puzzled.
"What I mean is, that we are likely to run aground upon some unknown island. If the shore is rocky, it may break us to pieces, and that, of course, will be attended with danger to life or limb."
Stubbs looked thoughtful.
"I should like to see land," he said, "but I wouldn't like to land in that way. It reminds me of an old lady who, traveling by cars for the first time, was upset in a collision. As she crawled out of the window, she asked, innocently: 'Do you always stop this way?'"
"There are dangers on land as well as on the sea," said the mate, "as your story proves; though one is not so likely to realize them. In our present circumstances, there is one thing I earnestly hope for."
"What is that?"
"That we may not have another storm. I fear, in her dismantled condition, the Nantucket would have a poor chance of outliving it, particularly as we have no one but Jack and myself to do seamen's work."
Mr. Stubbs walked thoughtfully away.
Harry, who had seen him talking with the mate, asked him what the nature of the conversation was.
Mr. Stubbs told him.
"The fact is, Harry," he said, "we are in a critical condition. Whether we are ever to see old terry firmy again"—Mr. Stubbs was not a classical scholar—"seems a matter of doubt."
"And the worst of it is," said Harry, "there seems to be nothing you or I can do to increase our chances of safety."
"No, unless we could manage to see a ship which the chief officer had overlooked. That, I take it, is not very likely."
It was toward morning of the fifth night after the captain had left the ship that all on board were startled by a mighty thumping, accompanied by a shock that threw the sleepers out of bed.
Harry ran hastily on deck. The mate was there already.
"What's happened, Mr. Holdfast?" asked the boy, anxiously.
"The ship has struck on a rocky ledge!"
"Are we in danger?"
"In great danger. Call all the passengers. We must take to the boat, for the Nantucket is doomed!"

CHAPTER XIV

THE WRECK OF THE NANTUCKET

It was still quite dark, but it was light enough to see that the ship had struck upon a reef. Straining their eyes, the alarmed passengers could descry land. Indeed, the reef was an outlying part of it.
All eyes were turned upon the captain, as Mr. Holdfast was now called.
"If I had had men enough to stand watch, this would not have happened," he said.
"Is there any hope, Mr. Holdfast?" asked Montgomery Clinton, clasping his hands in terror.
"Plenty of it," answered the mate, curtly, "but we must leave the ship."

Under his direction the remaining boat—for Captain Hill and his companions had only taken away one—was lowered. Steering clear of the reef, they found themselves in a cove, bordered on three sides by land. By the light, now rapidly increasing, they saw grass and trees, and the sight gladdened them in spite of the grave peril that menaced them.

They put in the boat as large a supply of stores as they dared, and then rowed ashore. Landing the passengers, Holdfast selected Jack and Harry, and went back to the ship for a further supply.

"We must lay in as much as we can, for we don't know how long we are to remain here," he said.

When the second trip had been made, it was decided to rest for a time and eat breakfast.

The little group gathered on a bluff looking out to sea, and, sitting down, ate heartily. By this time the sun had made its appearance, and it bade fair to be a pleasant day.

"Have you any idea where we are, Mr. Holdfast?" asked Mr. Stubbs.

"I only know that we are on an island. There is no mainland near here," answered the commander.

"It seems to be a large one, then. While you were gone with the boys, I ascended a tree, and, looking inland, could not see the ocean in that direction."

"I feel like exploring the island," said Harry; "who will go with me?"

Curious to see what kind of a new home they had, all set out. First, however, the professor asked:

"How long before the ship is likely to go to pieces, Mr. Holdfast?"

"Not under a day or two in this weather," was the answer. "Later in the day I will board her again."

They struck inland and walked for about two miles. There were trees and plants such as they had never seen before, and the songs of unknown birds floated out upon the air. It was certainly a delightful change from the contracted life they had been leading upon shipboard.

"Do you think the island is inhabited?" asked Harry.

"I know no more about it than you do, my lad," answered Holdfast.

"Suppose we should meet with a pack of savages armed with spears!" suggested Harry, with a side look at Clinton, who was walking by him.

"Oh, good gracious! Mr. Holdfast, do you think we will?" asked that young gentleman, nervously.

"We must do the best we can. I take it we are all brave, and would be willing to fight."

After a considerable walk, they reached a grove of trees, bearing a different leaf from any to which they were accustomed. They did not appear to produce fruit of any kind, but were comely and afforded a grateful shade. This was the more appreciated, because the sun had begun to make its heat felt, and a feeling of languor diffused itself over all.

"I move we squat here a while," said Mr. Stubbs.

"Very well," said the mate. "We have all day before us, and I am afraid a great many more to come, in which we may explore the island."

All threw themselves on the grass without ceremony.

They returned to the shore about noon, and sitting down on the bluff, ate heartily of the stores they had brought with them from the ship. They had brought no water, but, fortunately, discovered a spring on their homeward walk, which promised a constant supply of refreshing drink.

"This seems a great deal like a picnic," said Harry, as they sat down on the grass with the food in the center.

"I am afraid it will prove a larger picnic than we care for," remarked the professor.

When dinner was over, if their informal meal can be dignified by that name, Mr. Holdfast said:

"I think we had better make another trip to the ship, and bring back what we can. We shall need a further supply of provisions, and there will be other things that will occur to us as likely to be needed."

"May I go with you, Mr. Holdfast?" asked Harry.

"Yes," answered the mate; "I will take you and Jack, and Mr. Stubbs, too, may come, if he will."

"I am quite at your command, captain," said the Yankee.

Nothing suited Harry better than to make one of the expeditions. He and Jack clambered up the ship's sides, and chased each other in boyish fun. Jack had no fear of a stern rebuke from Mr. Holdfast, who had a sympathy with the young. He would not have dared to take such liberties with Captain Hill.

"How long do you think the ship will hold together, Mr. Holdfast?" asked Stubbs.

"For a week, perhaps, unless the sea becomes rough, and dashes her against the reef with violence."

"At present she seems motionless."

"Yes, she is not at present receiving any damage. It will be a sad day when she goes to pieces," continued the mate, gravely.

"Yes, but it will hardly make our position worse. There is no chance of our making any use of her, I take it."

"You don't quite understand me," said Holdfast. "A sailor gets to feel an attachment for the craft he sails on, and she seems to him something like a living creature. This is my first voyage on the old Nantucket, but it will grieve me to see her disappear."

It was not easy to decide of what the boat's load should consist. In the main, provisions were taken as an article of first necessity. Some clothing, also, was selected, and among the rest, at Harry's instance, an extra pair of Mr. Clinton's trousers.

It was decided not to make another trip to the ship that day. Mr. Holdfast expressed the opinion that the Nantucket was not in any immediate danger of going to pieces, and there was much other work in hand.

"Do you know anything about the climate here, Mr. Holdfast?" asked the professor.

"I don't think it is ever cold. It is too far south for that."

"I mean as to the chance of rain. I am told that in these tropical places, rain comes on very suddenly at times."

"I suspect that this is the dry season, professor."

"Still, it may be wise to provide ourselves with some shelter."

"True; have you anything to suggest?"

"It occurred to me that we might procure some of the sails, and use as a roof covering to shield us from the heat of the sun, and from any unexpected showers."

"A good idea. I am glad you mentioned it. On the whole, I think I will make one more trip to the ship this afternoon for the special purpose of bringing back materials for a roof. Then we can put it up to-night."

"Better bring hatchets, if there are any on board, some nails and cordage."

"Also well thought of. You are a practical man, professor."

"We shall all have to think for the general benefit. I am sorry I can't do more work, but I never was handy with tools."

"I am," said Stubbs. "In fact, most Yankees are, and I am a Yankee. You can command my services, Mr. Holdfast, in any way that you see fit."

Mr. Holdfast made another trip to the vessel, and brought back quite an expanse of sailcloth. All hands, with the exception of Mr. Clinton, went to work at once, and by sunset a considerable space was roofed over, which the little company regarded with complacency.

"Aren't you going to have any sides or doors?" asked Clinton.

"That can be considered hereafter," said Holdfast. "I don't think we shall need any, since the probability is that the island is not inhabited."

The next morning a great surprise awaited them.

It might have been because it was the first night on land, or perhaps because they were unusually fatigued, but at any rate the little party slept unusually late. The first one to awake was Harry Vane. It took very little time for him to dress, since he had only taken off his coat. He glanced at his slumbering companions, who were scattered about in different postures.

"I'll go up to the spring, and have a wash," Harry decided. "I won't wake anybody, for there's no hurry about waking up."

Returning from the spring, Harry for the first time looked in the direction of the ship. What he saw filled him with amazement. The wreck which he had thought deserted, was alive with men. He saw a dozen on deck, including two who were obviously not sailors. He could not immediately discern the figures, and ran hastily to the top of the bluff. Then he made the startling discovery that these intruders were the captain and his companions, who had abandoned the ship in the expectation that it was doomed, and, after floating about in the long boat, had by a wonderful coincidence drifted to the very point which they themselves had reached.

The news was too important to keep, and he returned to the encampment, and entering, approached the mate, who was sleeping soundly. He leaned over and shook him gently.

"Mr. Holdfast!" he cried.

The mate slowly opened his eyes and started up.

"What's the matter?" he asked. "Has anything happened?"

"I've got great news for you, Mr. Holdfast. Captain Hill has arrived."

"What!" exclaimed the mate, in amazement. "Arrived—where?"

"He is at this moment on the Nantucket, with all the men that accompanied him in the long boat."

Uttering an expression of amazement, Mr. Holdfast sprang from the ground, and hastily made his way to the edge of the bluff.

"By Jove!" said he, "you're right. I never heard of anything more wonderful."

Harry could not tell from the expression of his face whether he considered the news good or not.

"Go and wake up the rest, Harry," he said. "They will be surprised, too."

It is needless to say that the news produced surprise and excitement. All hurried to the edge of the bluff.

"Will they come on shore, do you think?" asked Harry of the mate.

"They will have to; but I shall at once go out to the ship and report to my superior officer. You and Jack may go with me."

It is needless to say that both boys were very glad to accept this invitation. The rest of the party remained on shore and watched the boat's course.

"What will be the issue of this, Mr. Stubbs?" asked the professor, thoughtfully.

"I am afraid there will be friction. The captain is a natural despot, and he will undertake to control us."

"He can have no authority after the ship is wrecked."

"He will claim it, as sure as my name is Stubbs. The fact is, I am rather sorry he hadn't managed to drift to another island. Mr. Holdfast is a much more agreeable man to deal with."

"I agree with you. As a passenger, I shall not recognize the captain's authority on shore."

"Nor I."

Meanwhile, the mate and the two boys had pulled to the ship, and, securing the boat, scrambled on deck.

"Good-morning, Captain Hill; I am glad to meet you once more," said the mate.

"Humph!" growled the captain, not over politely. "When did you reach here?"

"Yesterday morning."

"Where are the rest of the party?"

"We have a little camp just back of the bluff."

"I see you have been removing articles from the ship," continued the captain, in a tone of disapproval.

"Certainly," answered the mate. "We need them, and I didn't know how long the ship would last."

"It seems in no immediate danger of going to pieces."

"Things look more favorable than they did yesterday morning. What sort of a trip did you have in the boat?"

"A curious question to ask," said the captain, captiously. "We were in danger of being swamped more than once."

"We had better have remained on board the Nantucket with you, Mr. Holdfast," said Appleton, the Melbourne merchant.

Captain Hill chose to take offense at this remark.

"You were quite at liberty to stay, Mr. Appleton," he said. "I didn't urge you to go with me."

"True, Captain Hill; but I trusted to your opinion that the ship was unsafe."

The captain looked angry, but did not make any reply.

By the sailors Mr. Holdfast was warmly greeted. He was much better liked than the captain, being a man of even temper and reasonable in his demands.

CHAPTER XV

THE LAST OF THE "NANTUCKET"

Though the mate had removed some of the stores, much the larger portion was left on board, for the Nantucket had been provisioned for a long voyage. Yet Captain Hill saw fit to complain.

"It is fortunate that you didn't take all the stores, Mr. Holdfast," he remarked, in a sarcastic tone.

The mate eyed the captain steadily.

"May I ask your meaning, Captain Hill?" he asked.

"I mean what I say, sir. I think my language requires no interpreter."

"Then I can only reply that it would have made no difference if I had removed all the provisions."

"You appear to forget that I am your superior officer," said the captain in a heat.

"I had no superior officer at the time I ordered the removal."

"You have now, at any rate."

"We are not at sea, Captain Hill. The vessel is wrecked, and all distinctions are at an end. Now it is each for himself."

"So, sir, you defy my authority!" exclaimed the captain, looking black.

"I don't recognize it, that is all."

"You shall, sir!" retorted the captain, frowning. "You shall learn, also, that I have means to enforce it. I have nearly a dozen seamen under me, and you have only the boy, Jack Pendleton."

"Captain Hill, all this is very foolish. We are ship-wrecked, and have taken refuge on the same island. Instead of quarreling, we should help each other."

"So you presume to lecture me!" sneered the captain.

Mr. Holdfast didn't care to continue the dispute.

"I am ready to help you remove what you require," he said, quietly. "It will be well to remove as much as possible today, for we may at any time have a storm, that will effectually put an end to our work."

"Very well, sir; I am glad you show a better spirit."

The mate was both annoyed and amused at this evident intention to throw upon him the whole onus of the quarrel, but he did not care to reply. He and the two boys helped remove the stores, and it being quite early, by noon several boatloads had been deposited on shore, to be removed farther inland when there was a good opportunity. One thing Mr. Holdfast noted with apprehension. There was a considerable quantity of brandy and other spirits in the captain's cabin, which he took care to have included in the articles removed. Remembering the captain's weakness, he feared this might lead to trouble. But he did not take it upon himself to remonstrate, knowing that in the state of the captain's feelings toward him it would be worse than useless.

By three o'clock about all the stores, with other needful articles, had been removed, and there was a large pile on the bluff.

"Captain, will you walk over and see my encampment?" asked Holdfast, now that there was leisure.

"Lead on, sir," said the captain, though not overpolitely. It was not far away, and a short walk brought them in front of it.

"Perhaps you will feel inclined to settle near by," suggested Holdfast.

"No, sir; I don't care to intrude upon you."

Eventually the captain selected a spot about half a mile away. Here an encampment was made, very similar to the mate's but on a larger scale.

"I am glad the captain is not close alongside," said Jack Pendleton.

"So am I," answered Harry, to whom this remark was made. "We are better off by ourselves."

"He would be sure to interfere with us. I saw him scowling at me more than once this morning. You know he don't like me."

"Nor me, either, Jack. It will be well for both of us to keep out of his way."

To the great delight of Clinton, more of his "wardrobe," as he called it, was brought ashore. For this he was indebted to the good-natured persistence of Harry, who, though amused at the vanity of the young man from Brooklyn, felt disposed to gratify him in a harmless whim.

The two parties remained apart, the original company remaining with the captain, while four passengers and Jack Pendleton stayed with the mate. Captain Hill showed a disposition to claim Jack, but Holdfast said, quietly: "I think captain, Jack had better stay with me for the present, as he is company for Harry Vane."

The captain looked dissatisfied, but was too tired to remonstrate at that time. He went to his own encampment, and indulged in liberal potations of brandy, which had the effect of sending him to sleep.

That night a violent wind sprang up. It blew from the sea inland, and though it did not affect the ship-wrecked parties or their encampment seriously, on account of their being screened by the intervening bluff, it had another effect which a day or two previous might have been disasterous. The ill-fated Nantucket was driven with such force against the reef that the strength of its hull was overtaxed. When the mate went to the bluff in the morning to take an observation, he was startled to find in place of the wreck a confused debris of timbers and fragments of the wreck.

As the mate was surveying the scene of ruin, Jack and Harry joined him.

"Look there, my lads!" said Holdfast. "That's the last of the poor old Nantucket. She will never float again."

They had known this before, but it was now impressed upon their minds forcibly, and a feeling of sadness came over the three.

"That settles it," said Harry, giving expression to a common feeling. "We are prisoners on the island now, and no mistake."

"When we leave here, it won't be on the Nantucket, anyway," said Jack.

"It is lucky this happened after we had brought our stock of provisions ashore," said the mate.

"Let us go down and see what these kegs and boxes contain," suggested Harry.

So the three descended to the reef, and began to examine the articles thrown ashore. For the most part they were of little value, though here and there were articles that might prove useful.

"Couldn't we make a raft out of the timbers of the old ship?" asked Jack.

"That is worth thinking of, though a raft would not do for a long voyage," said Holdfast.

"No, but we might be picked up."

"When the captain's party is awake it will be well for us to haul the loose timbers up to a place of safety."

"Here's Clinton's trunk," said Harry, bending over and recognizing the initials. "Here is the name, 'M. C., Brooklyn.' He will be overjoyed. Suppose we take it up between us."

No opposition being made by Mr. Holdfast, the boys took the trunk up between them, preceding the mate. They had just reached the summit of the bluff.

"Put down that trunk!" said a stern voice.

Looking up, the boys saw that the speaker was Captain Hill.

The captain's face was of dull, brick-red, and it was clear that he had already been drinking, early as it was. Naturally the boys, on hearing his voice, put down the trunk in their surprise, but they maintained their position, one on each side of it. Of the two, Jack was the more impressed, having been one of the crew, and subject to the captain's authority on shipboard. Harry, as a passenger, felt more independent. Indeed, he was indignant, and ready to resist what he thought uncalled-for interference on the part of the captain.

"This is Mr. Clinton's trunk," he said. "We are going to carry it to him."

"Do you dare to dispute my authority?" roared the captain, his red face becoming still redder.

"I don't see what you have to do with the trunk," answered Harry, boldly.

"This to me!" shrieked the captain, looking as if he were going to have a fit of apoplexy. "Do you know who I am?"

"You were the captain of the Nantucket," said Harry, quietly.

The captain, notwithstanding his inebriated condition, did not fail to notice that Harry used the past tense.

"I am still the captain of the Nantucket, as I mean to show you," he retorted.

"Then, sir, you are captain of a wreck that has gone to pieces."

Captain Hill upon this looked at the fragments of the unfortunate ship, and for the first time took in what had happened.

"It doesn't matter," said he, after a brief pause, "I am in command here, and"—here he interpolated an oath—"I don't allow any interference with my authority."

"You are not captain of Mr. Clinton's trunk," said Harry, in a spirited tone. "Jack, let us carry it along."

This was too much for the captain. With a look of fury on his face, he dashed toward Harry, and there is no doubt that our hero was in serious danger. He paled slightly, for he knew he was no match for the tall, sinewy captain, and was half regretting his independence when he felt himself drawn forcibly to one side, and in his place stood the mate, sternly eyeing the infuriated captain.

"What do you want to do, Captain Hill?" he asked.

"To crush that young viper!" shouted the captain, fiercely.

"You shall not harm a hair of his head!"

By this time the captain's wrath had been diverted to the mate. He struck out with his right hand, intending to fell him to the ground, but, the mate swerving, he fell from the force of his abortive blow, and, being under the influence of his morning potations, could not immediately rise.

"Boys," said Mr. Holdfast, "you may take hold of the trunk again and go on with it. Don't be afraid. If the captain makes any attempt to assault you, he will have me to deal with."

Harry and Jack did as directed. Jack, however, could not help feeling a little nervous, his old fear of the captain asserting itself. But Harry, confident in the protection of his good friend, the mate, was quite unconcerned.

Mr. Holdfast walked on beside them.

"The captain seems disposed to make trouble," he said. "He fancies that he is captain of this island, as he was chief officer of the Nantucket. I shall convince him of his mistake."

"I hope you won't get into any trouble on my account, Mr. Holdfast," said Harry, considerately.

"Thank you, my lad; but Tom Holdfast doesn't propose to let any man walk over him, even if it is his old skipper. Now that the ship is gone, Captain Hill has no more authority here than I have."

As the captain fell, his head came in contact with a timber with such violence that, combined with his condition, he was forced to lie where he fell for over an hour.

As the boys emerged upon the bluff with the trunk, Clinton, who had just got up, recognized it, and ran up to them, his face beaming with delight.

"Oh, Mr. Vane!" he said, "have you really brought my trunk? You are awfully kind."

Then they had breakfast—a very plain meal, as might be supposed. Some of the sailors came over from the other camp, and one of them asked Mr. Holdfast if he had seen the captain.

"You will find him on the beach," answered the mate. "He has been carrying too much sail, I think," he added, dryly.

After a while the captain picked himself up, and gazed moodily at the wreck, of which so little remained. Then, the events of the morning recurring to him, he frowned savagely, and, turning toward the bluff, he shook his fist angrily in the direction of the mate's encampment.

CHAPTER XVI

CONCLUSION

Among the sailors was an Italian named Francesco. Probably he had another name, but no one knew what it was. In fact, a sailor's last name is very little used. He was a man of middle height, very swarthy, with bright, black eyes, not unpopular, for the most part, but with a violent temper. His chief fault was a love of strong drink. On board the Nantucket grog had been served to the crew; and with that he had been content. But at the time of the wreck no spirits had been saved but the captain's stock of brandy. Francesco felt this to be a great hardship. More than any other sailor he felt the need of his usual stimulant. It was very tantalizing to him to see the captain partaking of his private stock of brandy while he was compelled to get along on water.

"The captain is too mucha selfish," he said one day to a fellow-sailor. "He should share his brandy with the men."

Ben Brady, the sailor to whom he was speaking, shrugged his shoulders.

"I think I will try some of the captain's brandy when he is away," said Francesco, slyly.

"If you do, you will get into trouble. The captain will half murder you if he finds it out."

"He is not captain now—we are all equal—all comrades. We are not on ze sheep."

"Take my advice, Francesco, and leave the brandy alone."

Francesco did not reply, but he became more and more bent on his design.

He watched the captain, and ascertained where he kept his secret store. Then he watched his opportunity to help himself. It was some time before he had an opportunity to do so unobserved, but at length the chance came.

The first draught brought light to his eyes, and made him smack his lips with enjoyment. It was so long since he had tasted the forbidden nectar that he drank again and again. Finally he found himself overcome by his potations, and sank upon the ground in a drunken stupor.

He was getting over the effects when, to his ill-luck, the captain returned from his usual solitary ramble.

"He has been at my brandy!" Captain Hill said to himself, with flaming eyes. "The fool shall pay dearly for his temerity."

He advanced hastily to the prostrate man, and administered a severe kick, which at once aroused the half-stupefied man.

Francesco looked up with alarm, for the captain was a much larger and stronger man than himself.

"Pardon, signor captain," he entreated.

"You have been drinking my brandy, you beast," said Captain Hill, furiously.

I draw a veil over the brutal treatment poor Francesco received. When it was over he crawled away, beaten and humiliated, but in his eye there was a dangerous light that boded no good to the captain.

Presently Francesco began to absent himself. Where he went no one knew or cared, but he, too, would be away all day. His small, black eyes glowed with smoldering fires of hatred whenever he looked at the captain, but his looks were always furtive, and so for the most part escaped observation.

One day Captain Hill stood in contemplation on the edge of a precipitous bluff, looking seaward. His hands were folded, and he looked thoughtful. His back was turned, so he could not, therefore, see a figure stealthily approaching, the face distorted by murderous hate, the hand holding a long, slender knife. Fate was approaching him in the person of a deadly enemy. He did not know that day by day Francesco had dogged his steps, watching for the opportunity which had at last come.

So stealthy was the pace, and so silent the approach of the foe, that the captain believed himself wholly alone till he felt a sharp lunge, as the stiletto entered his back between his shoulders. He staggered, but turned suddenly, all his senses now on the alert, and discovered who had assailed him.

"Ha! it is you!" he exclaimed wrathfully, seizing the Italian by the throat. "Dog, what would you do?"

"Kill you!" hissed the Italian, and with the remnant of his strength he thrust the knife farther into his enemy's body.

The captain turned white, and he staggered, still standing on the brink of the precipice.

Perceiving it, and not thinking of his own danger, Francesco gave him a push, and losing his balance the captain fell over the edge, a distance of sixty feet, upon the jagged rocks beneath. But not alone! Still retaining his fierce clutch upon the Italian's throat, the murderer, too, fell with him, and both were stretched in an instant, mangled and lifeless, at the bottom of the precipice.

When night came, and neither returned, it was thought singular, but the night was dark, and they were unprovided with lanterns, so that the search was postponed till morning. It was only after a search of several hours that the two were found.

After the captain's death two distinct camps were still maintained, but the most cordial relations existed between them. At the suggestion of the mate, an inventory was made of the stock of provisions, and to each camp was assigned an amount proportioned to the number of men which it contained.

There was no immediate prospect of want. Still, the more prudent regarded with anxiety the steady diminution of the stock remaining, and an attempt to eke them out by fresh fish caught off the island. But the inevitable day was only postponed. At length only a week's provisions remained. The condition was becoming serious.

"What shall we do?" was the question put to Mr. Holdfast, who was now looked upon by all as their leader and chief.

Upon this the mate called a general meeting of all upon the island, sailors and passengers alike.

"My friends," he said, "it is useless to conceal our situation. We are nearly out of provisions, and though we may manage to subsist upon the fish we catch, and other esculents native to this spot, it will be a daily fight against starvation. I have been asked what we are to do. I prefer rather to call for suggestions from you. What have you to suggest?"

"In my view there are two courses open to us," said Mr. Stubbs, finding that no one else appeared to have anything to propose. "We must remain here and eat the rest of our provisions, but there seems very little chance of our attracting the attention of any passing vessel. We appear to be out of the ordinary course. Of course, it is possible that some ship may have passed the island without attracting our notice. What is your opinion, Mr. Holdfast?"

"The flag of the Nantucket, as you know, has floated night and day from a pole erected on a high bluff," said the mate. "The chances are that if any vessel had come sufficiently near it would have attracted attention, and led to a boat being lowered, and an exploring party sent thither."

"While we've got any provisions left," said the boatswain, "let us take the boats, and pull out to sea. We can go where the ships are, and then we'll have some chance. They'll never find us here, leastways, such is my opinion."

"My friends," said the mate, "you have heard the proposal made by the boatswain. All who are in favor of it will please raise their right hand."

All voted in the affirmative.

"My friends," said Mr. Holdfast, "it seems to be the unanimous sentiment that we leave the island, and sail out far enough to be in the course of passing vessels. I concur in the expediency of this step, and am ready to command one of the boats. Mr. Harrison will command the other."

"How soon shall we start?" asked a passenger.

"The sooner the better! To-morrow morning, if it is pleasant."

This decision pleased all. Something was to be done, and hope was rekindled in the breasts of all. Heretofore they had been living on, without hope or prospect of release. Now they were to set out boldly, and though there was the possibility of failure, there was also a chance of deliverance.

No sooner was the decision made than all hands went to work to prepare for embarking.

In the appointment of passengers, Mr. Holdfast, who commanded the long boat, retained Harry, the professor and Clinton. Six sailors, including Jack Pendleton, made up the complement.

"I am glad you are going to be with us, Jack," said Harry, joyfully. "I shouldn't like to be separated from you."

"Nor I from you, Harry," returned Jack.

At eight o'clock the next morning they started. As the island faded in the distance, all looked back thoughtfully at their sometime home.

Three days the boats floated about on the bosom of the ocean—three days and nights of anxiety, during which no sail was visible. But at length a ship was sighted.

"In one way or another we must try to attract attention," said the mate.

Not to protract the reader's suspense, let me say that by great good fortune the mate of the approaching ship, in sweeping the ocean with his glass caught sight of the two boats, and changed the course of the vessel so as to fall in with them.

"Who are you?" he hailed.

"Shipwrecked sailors and passengers of the ship Nantucket," was the answer of Mr. Holdfast.

They were taken on board, and discovered that the vessel was the Phocis, from New York, bound for Melbourne.

"We shall reach our destination after all, then, professor," said Harry, "and you will be able to give your entertainments as you at first proposed."

Professor Hemenway shook his head.

"I shall take the first steamer home," he said. "My wife will be anxious about me, and even now is in doubt whether I am alive or dead. You can return with me, if you like."

"No," answered Harry. "After the trouble I have had in getting to Australia, I mean to stay long enough to see what sort of a country it is. I think I can make a living in one way or another, and if I can't, I will send to America for the money I have there."

In due time they reached Melbourne, without further mischance. Harry induced Jack to remain with him, but Mr. Clinton, with a new stock of trousers, purchased in Melbourne, returned to America on the same steamer with the professor.

Here we leave Harry and Jack to pursue their course to such eminence as they may desire from the characteristics they have portrayed in this narrative.

THE END

Note from the Editor

Odin's Library Classics strives to bring you unedited and unabridged works of classical literature. As such, this is the complete and unabridged version of the original English text unless noted. In some instances, obvious typographical errors have been corrected. This is done to preserve the original text as much as possible. The English language has evolved since the writing and some of the words appear in their original form, or at least the most commonly used form at the time. This is done to protect the original intent of the author. If at any time you are unsure of the meaning of a word, please do your research on the etymology of that word. It is important to preserve the history of the English language.

Taylor Anderson

Made in United States
North Haven, CT
30 March 2025

67362673R00036